KILLED
ON THE
ROCKS

By the same author

KILLED ON THE ROCKS

William L. DeAndrea

THE MYSTERIOUS PRESS

New York • Tokyo • Sweden • Milan

Published by Warner Books

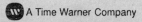 A Time Warner Company

MYSTERIOUS PRESS EDITION

Copyright © 1990 by William L. DeAndrea
All rights reserved.

The Mysterious Press name and logo are trademarks of Warner Books, Inc.

Cover illustration by Bobbye Cochran

Mysterious Press books are published by
Warner Books, Inc.
666 Fifth Avenue
New York, New York 10103
A Time Warner Company

Printed in the United States of America

Originally published in hardcover by The Mysterious Press.
First Mysterious Press Paperback Printing: November, 1991

10 9 8 7 6 5 4 3 2 1

1

. . . on the road in upstate New York.
—Charles Kuralt, "CBS Evening News
with Walter Cronkite" CBS

You might have thought the New York State Thruway was a three-hundred-mile-long runway, and the stretch Lincoln limousine a particularly inefficient airplane. The limo was so trunk-heavy, the nose of the thing pointed upward at a perceptible angle. The front wheels were so light on the asphalt that the driver was steering with one finger.

My contribution to the overload was one suitbag and one small suitcase. There had hardly been room for them. Fully half the trunk had been taken up with financial reports and "draft instruments," courtesy Charles R. Wilberforce, of the Network's Legal Department. The rest of it was filled up with *stuff*. Wintertime stuff. Fun stuff. Some of it belonged to Carol Coretti, Wilberforce's assistant, but most of it was the property of Roxanne Schick. Roxanne was the granddaughter of the founder of the Network, and the daughter of a past president.

In her early twenties, she was one of the richest women in the world.

She was also the Network's largest single stockholder,

1

though aside from depositing dividend checks, she hadn't had much to do with the family business before now.

She frequently said she hated the Network. She claimed the Network had been responsible for the various catastrophes that had befallen her family (father's death, mother's insanity, grandfather's suicide). She was not unjustified in making that claim. She *didn't* blame the Network for causing her to run away from home, and become hooked on drugs, walking the streets to support her habit, and I was proud of her for that. A lot of social-worker types would have let her get away with it, but accepting responsibility for her own actions was a big part of what had kept her straight all these years.

But this trip was one bit of company business that was not going to be allowed to take place in her absence. Not only was she going into seclusion with the rest of us at G. B. Dost's Adirondack retreat, she was treating it like a school trip. She was wearing corduroy slacks and a sweater with DEER knitted on it and a fake-fur-lined parka and a wool hat with a little pom-pom. Her eyes were bright, and she was bouncing on the seat beside me. I would say she looked like a fifteen-year-old, except I'd first met her when she was fifteen, and then she was a strung-out junkie, emaciated and damn near dead.

This was a decided improvement, I thought. Even if the reason for all this glee was that she was on her way to sell the Network.

Just north of Albany, where the Thruway runs into the Northway, Roxanne gasped, and grabbed my arm. "Cobb!" she cried.

Wilberforce looked up from a file he'd been reading. He had no expression on his face, but then he never did. His grayish-pink skin was on so tight, I didn't think he could move his face if he wanted to. It was a wonder he could talk.

Carol Coretti's face showed real concern. She was a tall

woman, auburn-haired, my age or a little older, with a pleasantly lupine face. She asked if something was wrong at the same time I said, "What's the matter, Rox?"

"We forgot your skis!"

Wilberforce went back to his file. He managed to radiate disgust, even if he couldn't show it. Carol Coretti smiled. I wondered how someone as nice as she seemed managed to survive daily contact with a fish like Wilberforce.

I turned to Roxanne. "No, we didn't," I said.

"Yes," she insisted. "I saw Ralph repacking the trunk when we picked you up." Ralph was the driver. "There were only two sets of skis and poles in there, mine and Miss Coretti's."

"Call me Carol," Carol said.

Wilberforce looked up from his paper for a second, just *daring* somebody to call him Charlie.

Roxanne declined the dare. "I already know Mr. Wilberforce didn't bring any skis."

"Yeah. Neither did I."

"Why not, Matt? Rocky Point has *two private downhill runs*, and a private lift. Do you know what that means? No lines. And it's been snowing up there on and off for weeks. The weather forecast calls for four to five inches of fresh powder."

"It's snowing now," Carol Coretti said.

I hooked a curtain aside with my finger and looked. It was indeed snowing, fat little powder puffs that hit the cold asphalt, then blew across the road like miniature tumbleweeds. That couldn't last—they'd start sticking to the road before too long. I hoped the limo and Ralph were up to it. The load in the trunk would be good for traction, at any rate.

Roxanne was delighted. She saw the snow only as a source of fun, not as an inconvenience, or even a driving hazard. I've noticed that skiers have a tendency to think that way.

"Oh," she said. "Look at it. Do you think it will be like that all the way up?"

"Ask Ralph to try to get a weather forecast on the radio," I suggested.

She ignored me. "I hope it is," she said. "Lots of fresh powder and no lines. I'm finally going to get as much skiing in as I want to."

"I've already gotten in as much skiing as I want to," I said.

Carol Coretti was suppressing a grin. "Have you had many bad skiing experiences, Mr. Cobb?"

"Matt," I said. "We're all on the same side here, right? But to answer your question, I have never had any bad experiences skiing, because I have never been skiing."

"But I thought you said—"

"Right. And that's exactly how much skiing I want to do in my life. None. I can feel my ankles snapping just watching 'Wide World of Sports.'"

"Cobb, I don't believe it," Roxanne said. "I've finally found something you're afraid of."

"You haven't been looking very hard."

"Well, I'm sure any place like Rocky Point is sure to have some equipment for guests. I'll teach you to ski, don't worry."

"I'm not worried. And neither you nor you assisted by a company of United States Marines is going to get a pair of those things on my feet. You ski. I'll build snowmen. Or better yet, I'll do some work. I'm getting paid for this, you know."

Without looking up from his papers, Wilberforce said softly, "Hear, hear."

My God, I thought. Wilberforce made a *joke*. We hadn't even arrived yet, and things were already getting weird.

2

All things are as they were then, except . . . *You Are There!*
—Walter Cronkite, "You Are There" (CBS)

This whole thing had started out to be fairly weird.

I had shown up for work one morning about a week earlier to find my secretary waving a message slip at me.

"Mr. Falzet wants to see you," she sang. The last word of the sentence wasn't quite "joo." Jasmyn Santiago had been a child when her family fled Cuba, but she still had the tiniest trace of an accent. She had a lot more of a trace of a stern, Hispanic-Catholic sense of the rightness of things, and she's always scolding me about not sharing it. She's younger than I am, and looks like a fashion model (she once told me she gets up at 5:00 A.M. to do her makeup), but the person in the world she reminds me of most is my grandmother.

"What's the matter?" I demanded. "Am I late again? It's got to be before nine o'clock." It's a talent I have. Under any circumstances, ask me what time it is, and I'll tell you correct to the nearest ten minutes. In my entire life, it had come in handy once. This time, on the defensive, I looked

5

at my watch. I showed it to Jazz. "See? Eight fifty-seven and a couple of seconds."

She wouldn't look. She closed her eyes and shook her head. "I don't care," she said. "When your boss gets in before you do, you are late."

Mmmm, I thought. A fairly stringent requirement. I tried to think of an occasion on which I'd beaten Jazz to the office, but couldn't. There had been times I'd stayed in Net HQ overnight, but I don't think they counted.

I decided to change the subject. "What the hell does Falzet want, anyway?"

Tom Falzet was president of the Network, and had been since Walter Schick's ultimately fatal accident. If I had to make a list of The Ten Most Obnoxious People I have ever known, Tom Falzet would take up the first six places on it. My name would occupy at least as big a percentage of *his* list.

We managed to do our jobs and avoid each other. The only reason he ever wants to see me is to rip off a piece of my hide, and the only time he ever feels safe doing that is when we're in the middle of some Network-threatening crisis. He feels safe then because handling crises for the Network is my job. I'm vice-president in charge of Special Projects. "Special Projects" is the title some nameless propaganda genius gave years ago to the part of the Network that would handle everything too nasty for the Legal Department, and too sensitive for Public Relations. If the wholesome star of one of our family sitcoms is strung out on dope, we'll try to keep it quiet while he gets straightened out. If he doesn't get straightened out, we'll arrange some other kind of reason for him to leave the show. That kind of thing. I'd never lusted after the job, and sometimes I didn't want it now, but I had it, and I did the best I could. I tried to keep things as legal as necessary and as moral as possible.

The reason Falzet is afraid the rest of the time to make

my life the living hell he thinks I deserve is that he's afraid I will use my influence with Roxanne Schick to screw *him* over. He's safe. I fight my own battles. But he doesn't have to know that.

I didn't rush upstairs in answer to Falzet's summons, but I didn't dawdle, either. There isn't too much to dawdle over in that building. The architect who'd built the place had decreed a stark, black-and-white decor, with no decorations in the hallways except for exit signs. It's a running joke around the Network that one of biggest health hazards of working at the place was snow blindness.

The elevator was brushed aluminum. Riding in it was like being inside a cigar tube. I took it all the way to the top, the thirty-seventh floor, and told the receptionist that Mr. Falzet was expecting me.

"Yes, Mr. Cobb," she said. Her eyes said, "Abandon hope, all ye who enter here."

I put on a brave face and walked in.

Falzet's office is enormous. It takes up the entire floor of the building. Some executives use their offices as putting greens. If he wanted to, Falzet could play a par-four hole of golf in his.

As always, he sat behind a polished ebony desk as big as a grand piano, watching me cross the room. I told him once that anyone could tell he was a big shot because there was nothing on his desk but a telephone.

As I walked across the expanse of black carpet, Falzet kept staring at me. Every once in a while, I had to go down or up a few stairs, which the architect had undoubtedly put in to keep the office from looking like an abandoned bowling alley.

Falzet is in his late fifties, a good-looking man in a big-toothed, horsey kind of way. He has the slightest trace of a southern accent. When I had crossed enough of his office to draw within earshot, he said, "Good morning."

This was a far cry from his usual greeting to me ("What

is the meaning of this"). It made me take a closer look at him.

This was a surprise, too. He wasn't angry. He wasn't happy, but he wasn't angry. Worried was more like it.

"Sit down, Cobb, sit down." This, too, was virtually unprecedented. I plunked myself down in a matte-finish black leather chair and waited for what might come next.

"What I'm about to tell you is a secret, Cobb."

"I've always treated all our, ah, conversations as confidential."

"Good. This one, even more so."

"All right."

Falzet took a deep breath. Whatever it was, it tasted bad enough to make him want to keep it off his tongue. Finally, he just spat it out all at once.

"The Network is a takeover target," he said.

"Oh," I said. "Well, there have been rumors ever since the other three went."

It was true. Over the past few years, the other major networks had been "acquired," as they say in the brokerage ads. ABC was swallowed by a smaller company called Capital Cities (business does not obey the laws of physics), NBC merged with General Electric—actually, reunited with them, since GE was one of the companies that founded NBC back in the twenties. The three-note bong *bong* bong signature NBC has used for years is g-e-c, standing for General Electric Corporation.

Where was I? Oh, right. Acquisitions. CBS, facing possible hostile takeovers, had found a white knight in the person of Lawrence Tisch, who had megabucks from the Loew's theater chain and other businesses, and who was a good friend of CBS founder and chairman William Paley.

Now, I am the owner of a few dozen shares of Network stock—some I bought on purpose, and some that were bestowed on me from time to time by virtue of my being a vice-president—but Big Business and High Finance are beyond me. I'm the kind of person who figures it's less wearing to take the bank's word for what my balance is at the end of the month than it is to do all that arithmetic.

Still, I had the occasional lunch with Betsy McCarren from the Finance Department, and I had long elevator rides with some of the Network's big money men, and I had picked up a hint or two.

One thing I'd gleaned is that the world of big business is as prone to fashion as a suburban high school. There was a time when, if you owed money, you were in debt, and were to be avoided at all costs. Now, if you owe enough, you are said to have used "leverage," and people ooh and ahh about how smart you are. And just like the year everybody in the building I live in bought a VCR, the current trend in the financial world was to buy or sell a TV network, depending, of course, on whether you already owned one.

The psychology of fashion was at work in the business world even more strongly on this one, because unlike VCRs, TV networks are always in limited supply. Rupert Murdoch's Fox Network was too new for him to want to sell, and too small to be a satisfying meal for a Wall Street shark. The other networks had already been eaten.

That left us.

"Who wants to buy us?" I asked hopefully. "Ted Turner?"

Falzet blanched. Apparently Turner had the same effect on him that Falzet usually had on me.

"My God, Cobb, don't even think that! The last thing—" He stopped. He looked at me with something close to panic in his eyes. "You haven't heard anything, have you?"

I almost laughed. I had made a point of irritating the man for such a long time, it was something very close to a habit. I decided not to, for two reasons. One, he was being amazingly civil, for him, and two, he was *really scared* over this.

"Nonono," I said. "This is the first I've heard about anything, beyond vague rumors."

"Then why did you say what you did?"

"Just speculating. I thought maybe if Turner bought the Network, he could colorize the building."

Falzet was bitter. "You may find the situation a fit matter for jokes, Cobb, but there's nothing funny about it. This is a billion-dollar corporation, in a government-regulated industry, with responsibilities and opportunities unlike those of any other sort of business. We have stockholders to protect, and a public trust to be true to."

"Yes, sir," I said. One of the reasons I still worked for the Network was that for all he was a petty tyrant and a major pain in the ass, Tom Falzet honestly believed all that stuff. More than that, he was honest, period. In this day and age, that was refreshing.

"Negotiations," he went on, "will be extremely delicate, and must be handled with the exact same care the government would give to nuclear-arms talks."

Well, I thought, all good things must come to an end. It had been ten minutes or so since I'd entered the room, and Falzet hadn't hit one of my linguistic pet peeves until just now. "The exact same" doesn't mean "exactly the same." If it means anything, it means "The same that has been taken away." I know it's a losing battle, but that doesn't mean I have to like it.

"With whom?" I said. I don't usually say "whom," but being with Falzet always makes me watch my grammar.

He begged my pardon.

"With whom are these negotiations to be held?" I asked, maybe overdoing it a little.

"Dost," he said.

"Ah," I said. I mentioned picking things up from financial people around the Network, but I could have known who G. B. Dost was just from looking at the headlines on other people's newspapers in the subway.

The headlines called him "Gold" Dost; his friends, legend had it, were instructed to call him Gabby. He first attracted national attention (translation: that's when I first heard of him) about ten years ago when he made several hundred million dollars for *not* buying an oil company. I remember thinking at the time that the oil company had been robbed. *I* would have not bought them for a measly fifty million or so.

In any case, Dost was what people liked to call a corporate raider. He bought companies the way a kid bought baseball cards, and treated them that way, too: collecting them, trading them, rearranging them, and for all I know, flipping them against other corporate raiders, to see who could get his company closest to the stoop without touching, winner take all.

There were strong rumors that Dost was so crooked that when he died, they were going to have to screw him into the ground. There were equally strong rumors that the Wall Street establishment, the prep school to Hahvud or Wharton business school to The Firm, the "I work on the Street because *Dad* worked on the Street" crowd, were out to get him because he had risen like a dust storm (a Dost storm) on the Montana prairie, and had parlayed some cows into a fortune that the Wall Streeters couldn't afford not to pay attention to.

I thought I knew what was eating Falzet. The Network's current Chairman of the Board was a former Air Force General who had been a good friend of the founder, Roxanne Schick's grandfather. He was a nice old man, and no dummy, but he was perfectly content to let Falzet have all the power as long as the profits stayed up, while he worked on his memoirs.

The General, at least, seemed destined for a golden handshake if the sale went through. Even if Falzet were to be kept around (and there was absolutely no reason why he shouldn't be—even with viewership for commercial TV

11

down, the Network and the Corporation that surrounded it were positively coining money), he would never have the free hand under Dost that he had currently.

"Where do I come into all this?" I asked. I suspected I wasn't going to like the answer.

"What do you mean?"

"I mean, if you expect me to quash the deal, you've come to the wrong place. It's not my kind of job; not Special Projects' kind of thing, either."

"Are you out of your mind?"

"You don't want me to quash the deal?"

"Absolutely not! Dost will bring a flood of new capital to the Network. He'll clean out the deadwood. There are big changes going on in this industry, Cobb. Cable is getting stronger all the time. New technologies. Possible deregulation. In five more years, the industry will be practically unrecognizable.

"But the board is loaded with fossils. Just because we're making money now, they expect it to go on forever! They expect *me* to make it go on forever, without changing anything. A Dost administration will fix that."

"You've been talking to his people already, I see."

"Well, ah, yes. Strictly preliminary, strictly theoretical. The formal offer will be made to the board after our people discuss some concretes with Dost."

"I wouldn't be much help trying to put the deal across, either."

"That won't be necessary. The takeover will make all their shares skyrocket in value. That alone should put it across."

"I still don't see why you need me."

"I need you because someone *else* is trying to quash the deal."

"Mr. Falzet, I'm trying to get across to you that no matter what shape these financial dealings take, I'm not the one to help you with them."

"Dammit, Cobb, I know we don't like each other, but you don't have to act like I'm a complete idiot! I know just what you're good for and what you're not. Believe me, the quashing that's been going on fits directly in with your field of expertise."

He opened a desk drawer, pulled out a manila folder, reached across the desk and handed it to me. "Look at that," he said.

It was a letter. A photocopy, not an original. It was addressed to Sandy Vath, director of the pension fund of International Radio and Television Employees, which was the union that represented the technicians and support personnel here at the Network. In an inspiring display of self-confidence, the union had been buying stock in the Network since they'd organized the place back in the forties. They now owned enough stock to put their man on the board. A lot of the old-line, cigar-chomping, anti–New Dealers on the board (and believe me, we had them) found Sandy Vath, to their surprise, to be levelheaded and easy to work with, instead of the bomb-throwing anarchist they'd probably been expecting. They were terribly disappointed.

Falzet's attitude was similar. He seemed to get along with Vath better than he did with the rest of the gang. Vath respected and trusted Falzet, which was probably how Falzet had wound up with a copy of this letter.

You can't tell as much from a copy as you can from an original, of course, but looking at this, I'd say it was done on a nice, anonymous laser printer. There was no date. The letter itself was short and to the point.

Dear Mr. Vath:
    G. B. Dost is planning to buy the Network. Do not let him. There is insanity in the man and all those around him. There is treachery. There is murder. He will soon

destroy himself; he will destroy your Network with him, if you let it happen.

The letter begged for a signature like *"A friend"* or *"One who knows,"* but there was nothing.

"Okay," I said. "You win. This is our territory."

"I thought you'd feel that way."

I nodded. Falzet was the one who had to worry about new technologies and the changing face of the industry. I only had to worry about human weakness and nastiness, and that never changed.

3

. . . the mystery of . . . Cliff House!
—Sonny Bono, "The Sonny and Cher Show" CBS

There was no mystery about why the place was called Rocky Point. For one thing, it was about two thirds of the way up a mountain, on an overgrown cliff sticking out of the south side. I know any Westerners reading this are chortling now—they always chortle at what we Easterners refer to as a mountain. Tough. Believe me, if you fell off the top of Mount Sumac, or even from as high up as Rocky Point, you would be just as dead when you hit as if you fell off Mount Everest.

There were also plenty of rocky points hanging around. The whole curving road up the mountain was lined with them on the outer lane. The motif continued even when we hit the level place where the mansion was built, a rough rectangle about the size of a football field. Rocky Point (the house) was built on about the far forty yard line, so that there was a big yard in front of it, leading to the rest of Mount Sumac, and a smaller area behind, leading up to a sheer drop of about nine hundred feet.

The pointed black rocks lining the drive up to the house

were mostly covered by snow, now. The "fresh powder" had gone well past the predicted four-to-five inches, and showed no signs of stopping. It looked as if there was an enormous conga line of sharks just below the surface. I wouldn't have wanted to drive across that plateau once they were all covered. The road was by no means straight, and the rocks were just the right height to gut a car completely if you happened to drive across them.

With the snow, it had taken us about three hours longer to get there than we'd originally planned. Roxanne was fatalistic about it.

"There's the lift," she said. To our left was a chair lift that headed up the mountain. It was not in operation at the moment. "I guess it's too late to think about getting in any skiing today."

"Especially since it's going to be pitch black in about forty-five minutes," I said. "Let's just thank God and the limousine agency that Ralph is such a good driver and get unpacked."

I could see Ralph's grin in the mirror. A good driver is not supposed to talk to the passengers unless directly addressed, but Ralph had earned the right to bend protocol a little.

"All in a day's work, sir," he said.

The road led right to an eight-car garage. We filled up the eighth spot, obviously the last to arrive. There was a short flagstone walk between the garage and the house. Someone had shoveled it and salted it like bacalao, so it was passable. We zipped up our parkas and stepped outside.

Under the proper circumstances, I like snow. I liked it now. The air was so cold and clean it felt as if it were scouring my city-blackened lungs pink again, and the snow danced in the floodlights on the path. I stood for a few seconds in the dark gray twilight and looked at the house.

It was fabulous. Huge, built of limestone no doubt dug

out of these very mountains, with turrets and gables and all sorts of solemn Victorian doodads, Rocky Point was a house built to be haunted. Looking at the place, I could understand for the first time in my life why people who had, say, tens of millions of dollars felt it necessary to press on until they had hundreds of millions and then billions of dollars. They did it so that when there was a chance to buy something like Rocky Point, they could write a check and have it.

It was the kind of place where time stood still. The lights in the windows could have been candles or gas. Washington Irving could have been in one of them, watching the snow falling. If you turned your back to the ski lift, the only concession to modernity was the thick bunch of wires that ran from the northwest corner of the fourth floor, through the branches of a towering pine, and up over the crest of the mountain.

Wilberforce offered Roxanne his arm. She smiled prettily and took it. My God, I thought. First Falzet, now him. I was surrounded by humans. Having seen that, I could do no less than offer my arm to Carol Coretti. As she took it, she leaned close to me and spoke softly in my ear.

"Don't worry," she said. "He's only doing it because she's the major stockholder."

"He never struck me as the gallant type."

"Me neither," she said. "Believe me, if Ralph hadn't already started unloading things to the service entrance, Wilberforce would have had me carrying the cartons of papers."

The door was open by the time Carol and I got to the steps. Standing in the doorway was G. B. Dost, himself.

"Afraid you weren't going to make it, there, for a while. Kept listening to the radio, hearing about accidents. None with a limo in it, though. Come in, come in."

Dost stepped aside and waved us through the door into a high-ceilinged, timbered room with shields and animal heads all over the place. A flagstone hearth that must have been eight feet high and twice that wide roared fire from the other side of the room.

"Like to have a fire going on a snowy night," he said. "Atmosphere. Same reason I keep the animal heads here. Guy who built this place was a bloodthirsty cuss. The only thing I ever shot was a Chinese Red in Korea, '51, and I don't think I hurt him too bad. Hi! I'm Gabby Dost."

He shook hands with each of us, a vigorous, two-handed pump job; complimented Roxanne and Carol on their looks; told Wilberforce and me he was glad to meet us; helped a tall, bald-headed guy wearing a plaid shirt and suspenders ("This is Norman, he and his wife will be looking after us all") take our coats; and led us to the bottom of a vast marble staircase, where we were met by a gray-haired lady in a gray dress ("Mrs. Norman. Best cook in these hills").

"Agnes will see you to your rooms, now," Dost said. "Heat's on, so you should thaw out in no time. Dinner's easy and informal tonight, but it'll be good."

"Mr. Dost?" I said.

"Dress comfortable. No business tonight."

"Mr. Dost?"

"Call me Gabby, son. We'll just get to know each other tonight—"

"Gabby!" I yelled.

I startled him; he had to take a breath. There was an opening of maybe a hundredth of a second, and I stepped into it.

"My dog was in the car with the other Network people. Did he get here okay?"

"That your dog? Fine animal. Looking to sell him?"

"He's not really—"

"No? Don't blame you. A good dog, you can't put a price on him. Anyway, don't worry. He's been fed, and he's run around in the snow—he loved that—and he's been dried off, and the last I knew he was asleep in your room. Bring him down with you at suppertime, I'd like to better my acquaintance with the little guy."

"Some other time," I smiled. "Wilberforce is a little nervous around dogs."

"No," Dost said. "Poor fella."

As if you didn't know, I thought. I was beginning to like Gabby Dost quite a bit. I had to remind myself that even if I weren't here looking for signs of insanity, treachery, and murder, I'd still be honor bound to try to make it possible for Wilberforce and the gang to get the best possible deal out of him.

"I've got dogs out at the ranch, of course. I bring 'em here when I come in the summer. Man's life doesn't seem complete without a dog, somehow."

"Sometime after dinner," I said, "come on up to my room, and we'll have a real session with Spot. He is quite a dog."

"Sounds good. And maybe you and me can have a little personal talk, too."

"Suits me fine," I said.

In fact, it suited me better than fine. This was obviously one of the most gregarious men on the planet, and I had been wondering how I was going to get him alone. As I rushed up the stairs to catch up with Mrs. Norman and the rest of my traveling companions, I was congratulating myself on how easy clearing that first hurdle had been.

I'd seen from outside that Rocky Point had five stories below the roof line, and, as I found climbing the stairs, they were *tall stories*, twenty-four stairs each. I was hoping that Dost didn't plan to put us all on the fifth floor so we could be impressed with the view.

I heard voices up the next flight of stairs. So much for lodgings on the second floor.

I caught up with them on the third floor. Mrs. Norman was just showing Carol Coretti into her room. Roxanne had apparently already been stashed. Wilberforce and I waited in the hallway listening to the housekeeper's murmuring voice explaining the room. It seemed to take a long time.

Mrs. Norman came out of the room, looked back in and said, "Dial six on the phone by your bed if you want anything, dear." She turned to us and smiled, a nice motherly smile. Wilberforce seemed to shrink from it.

"Now, gentlemen," she said, and led us back the way we came. Our rooms were on the other side of the hall. Wilberforce first. She led him in, and there was more murmuring. When Mrs. Norman came out, her smile had turned rueful, and she was shaking her head. "We've got to get some good country cooking into him."

"Good luck," I said.

Then she led me into my accommodation. To say it was a "room" was to say a Rolls-Royce Corniche is a "car."

Except for the high ceiling, you would not have believed that this interior went with the outside of the building—or with the room with the fireplace and the stairs and hallways, either. They had been stately, imposing. This was opulent.

The rug was a golden-beige plush, so soft it didn't have to be any flashy color to get your attention. The furniture seemed to be (I'm no expert) genuine antiques, scrupulously maintained.

The bed was a work of art, a mahogany number big enough to use for a game of platform tennis, or any number of other sports. It had a spread of violet velvet, with a matching canopy.

Spot came bounding out of what must have been the bathroom as soon as I closed the door. I was glad to see him, and he, for a change, wasn't punishing me for leaving him with strangers for an extended period. When he jumped up in the air to lick my face, I found out why. His tongue and muzzle were ice cold.

"Been drinking out of the toilet, haven't you?" Spot is a pedigreed, purebred Samoyed, the offspring and father of champions. He was born in a mansion, and raised in the palatial Central Park West apartment of his true owners—Rick and Jane Sloan, a couple of extraordinarily wealthy friends of mine from college—but he has the manners of a slob.

Some people have chalked it up to my influence—while my parents weren't poor, "palatial" was not the first word that sprang to mind when I remembered the neighborhood I grew up in.

But, poor or not, my parents were very strict about manners. Spot did not learn how to drink out of toilet bowls from *me*.

I'd had custody of Spot for the past several years, while the Sloans kept financing and going along on expeditions (to hot and humid places where Americans are less than popular) to dig for ruins. I'd decided they wouldn't come back to New York until the place finally collapsed in a heap. Which, of course, could be any day now.

While they were gone, I watched Spot and had the use of their apartment, which might very well be described as palatial. It was only long exposure to their place that kept me from goggling at this one.

I checked out the bathroom. Whoever was responsible for the furnishing of this place had not financed the bedroom by economizing on the plumbing.

I ruffled Spot's cloud of pure white fur. "That's the way, boy," I said. "If you must drink out of a toilet, a marble one with a gold handle is the way to go." The sink was also marble and gold, as was the bath. If Roxanne's room was anything like mine (and, according to our relative importance in the scheme of things, it ought to be *better*) and she didn't get enough time to ski, she could make up for lost exercise by taking a few laps around the tub.

Dinner tonight was to be "casual." That's a word that

means different things to different people. I threw my bag on my bed, opened it, laid out a pair of gray slacks, a button shirt with a small blue check, a black sweater, a red tie, and a corduroy jacket. This was my "casual" outfit—any part of it could be ditched down to shirt and slacks to adjust to whatever the prevailing notion of "casual" at a given gathering happened to be.

Then I closed the bag and stuck it in a closet bigger than the first apartment I'd rented in Manhattan. I hate to unpack. I hate any kind of work that's done simply to be undone later.

I took a quick hot shower in the shower stall in the corner of the bathroom (more marble and gold) to get rid of the sticky feeling traveling for more than an hour always gives me. I remembered to lower the lid of the toilet before I left the room. I'd have to remember to ask for a more suitable water dish for Spot.

I dressed in the slacks and shirt, then explored the room in greater detail. Spot, having ascertained I was still alive and still interested in him, was now zonked out on the rug. As usual, he had chosen a major traffic lane, and I had to be careful not to step on him as I roamed around.

I stopped roaming when I found the TV. It was very cleverly hidden inside a massive piece of mahogany that I was calling a chifforobe, since my father had had something similar, if smaller, and that's what he'd called his. When I opened up the door, though, a 30-inch Sony color monitor rolled out on a double shelf. Just below it was a VCR. Sitting demurely on top was a universal remote.

It's a matter of honor for us Network executives to check the reception on the local affiliate whenever we find ourselves somewhere new. I pushed a couple of buttons.

The reception was fine. The reception on everything was fine. We were plugged into a cable system, and a damned good one. I pushed the plus button, and had

identified maybe thirty stations and cable ﬧ.
there was a knock on the door.

I still wasn't enough at home in this place to yeℏ
in." Besides, I'd bolted the door behind me when I'd cℴ
in. Force of habit.

I walked to the door and opened up for Gabby Dost.

"I figure this is as good a time for our little talk as any,"
he said. "Mind if I come in?"

4

Who knows what evil lurks in the hearts of men?
— Orson Welles (and others), "The Shadow" (MBS)

Dost asked me how I liked my room and sat down in an antique chair. I contented myself with a corner of the bed. It didn't sag. I love firm mattresses.

"It's beautiful," I told him. "It leads to two conflicting ideas, though."

"How's that?"

"The place wasn't like this when you bought it, was it?"

"Hell, no, it was a wreck. Took me more money to fix it up and furnish it than it did to buy it. Aranda handled the decorating. She's my wife. Really did some job, didn't she?"

"It's beautiful," I said again.

Dost laughed. "Son, don't bullshit a bullshitter. It looks like God's personal whorehouse, and I know it. But it looks like it cost *money*. When I bring people here—this is my official conference center, you know—whether it's my own people or somebody I'm negotiating with, I want this room to put them in the proper frame of mind."

"Which is?"

"Which is, we're playing in the big leagues. We can

spend more on a crapper than most people spend on a car and not give a damn because the amounts I deal with make that kind of money insignificant. It's like one time I was getting an honorary doctorate at Montana State—what the hell, it ain't Harvard, but they don't *like* me at Harvard—I heard these two science guys arguing. One of them was saying the earth was going to come to an end in five million years, and this other guy was saying nonono, it's five *billion* years, and they went on like that for an hour, as if either one of them was going to be around to have a laugh on the other dummy for getting it wrong. The point is, *it don't make any difference*.

"Besides, the whole remodeling job was a tax write-off as a business expense. But I do go on. You were saying something about two conflicting ideas."

"Yeah," I said. I had had a third idea in the meantime. The secret of Dost's success was simply never to let anyone else ever say anything except when he was damned good and ready. But I noticed something else, too. He'd been eager to talk to me, and he was certainly living up to his nickname, but he had not come within a mile of anything that could be called a point. I might have to yell at him again.

"Yeah, Gabby," I went on. "Seeing what you've done to this place, I was inclined to wonder if you had any money left to buy the Network with—"

"I just explained that. Besides—"

I talked right through him. "On the other hand, if you could do this without blinking, maybe we just ought to forget about negotiations and banks and the government and let you buy the Network cash on the barrelhead."

Dost laughed. He laughed loud and long, much louder and much longer than the line deserved. He laughed until tears came to his eyes.

"Gabby," I said.

He caught his breath and said, "Yes, Cobb?" I was so

26

astonished to see he was giving me time to go on, I almost forgot to.

"Don't bullshit a bullshitter," I said at last. "You know about the letter, don't you?"

"What letter is that?" He wasn't laughing, now.

"Come on. You're the one who wanted to have this talk. I don't think you sprinted upstairs to my room while my hair was still wet from the shower to ask me again if Spot is for sale."

Dost scratched his chin. "No. No, I didn't do that. He is a fine animal, though. Fella who brought him said to ask you why he's called Spot."

I had known this was coming, I had just hoped that the question would be asked at the dinner table or something, so I'd only have to deliver Rick Sloan's joke once.

"He's named," I said, "for the gigantic white spot that covers his entire body."

"Ah," he said. "A joke."

"You're changing the subject again. Are you or are you not aware that someone has sent letters to the Network's entire board of directors accusing you of insanity, treachery, murder and suicidal tendencies?"

"They forgot to mention dandruff and fallen arches."

"All right," I said. "With all due respect, Mr. Dost, to hell with you. Since this is your place, I can hardly throw you out of the room, but boy, I'd like to. I can't leave because of the snow. So as long as you're here, what would you like to watch on TV?"

Dost waved a big veined hand. "Oh, anything, anything. Never had TV up here until last week. Jack Bromhead supervised it. Great guy, Jack is, known him since our wildcat days. You'll meet him later. How's the reception?"

"Terrific. See for yourself."

"I decided if we were going to work out details on my buying a TV network, we might as well have TV around while we did it. That's deductible too, of course."

"Of course," I said. I pushed buttons on the remote. "'Jeopardy' okay?"

Dost narrowed his eyes at me, but said nothing for maybe two whole minutes, probably a record. The only sound was me beating the pants off tonight's contestants.

Dost spoke with the first commercial. "I'm not used to being spoken to that way." Not insulted or anything; just stating a fact.

"As much as you talk, I doubt you're used to being spoken to at all."

"When I buy the Network, I'll be your boss."

"I can hardly wait. I've gotten more cooperation out of a broken shoelace than I have from you."

"How much money do you make?"

"You find that out when you buy the Network."

Dost started to laugh. This time, it was real laughter, not the clownish hysterics he'd tried before. "Listen," he said. "This isn't the first company I've bought, you know. I'll bet I can tell you how much you make." He named a figure. "Is that about the number?"

"No," I said. Then I started to laugh. "That's exactly the number." I shook my head. "You're good."

"You're good, too, son. You know, I suspect I have dished out more bullshit than any man my age in the history of American business. Not lies, mind you. Just stuff that floats easy on the ear, stuff I say because I think somebody might like to hear it, or to fill up the air with syllables so I've got no time to say anything it would be smarter not to say."

He slapped his right knee. "But you don't go for it! And, more important, you won't stand for it, even from somebody as rich as me. I like that."

"It's not so much," I told him. "I'm not that crazy about my job, and I have free housing. There's not that much for me to lose."

Dost grinned. "I can fix that."

I asked him what he was talking about.

"Come work for me," he said.

"As soon as you buy the Network, I *will* be working for you. You said so yourself."

"Not like that. I mean, come work for me, personally. I'll pay you a whole lot more than what you're getting now, and you'll be able to get in on all the deals I make."

"Get thee behind me, Satan," I told him.

"What?"

"This is really improper, Gabby. I'm here as part of the team protecting the interests of the Network stockholders, and you're offering me a king's ransom."

"I never thought of it that way," he said.

"I'll bet. You're trying to con me with the brash-young-guy-shoots-off-to-billionaire-and-gets-job-offer-because-billionaire-likes-his-spunk scenario."

"No, really. I was just impressed by you, you know. Of course, what I did would be a lot more improper if you were actually one of those people who were involved in negotiations."

"Yeah," I said. "Which brings us back to the letter."

"Yeah," he echoed. "The letter. Okay, I've seen it."

"At last!" I moved to turn the TV off.

"Wait. Might as well see final 'Jeopardy'."

"I thought you hardly ever watch TV."

"I didn't say I never watch it."

The answer came up: "These two actors won Oscars in the '70s for playing the same character."

"Got me," he said.

"Who were Marlon Brando and Robert DeNiro?" I said. "Can I turn off the TV, now?"

"Sure," he said. "A movie question. I hardly ever get to the movies, either."

"Who showed you the letter?"

"A friend."

"On the board?"

"Of course on the board. I've got friends on your board. I've got friends on lots of boards. How do you think I know when a company's ready to change hands?"

"So tell me the name of the friend."

"Why?" Gabby was showing me he could be terse when he wanted to.

"Because the purpose of the letter is to break up the takeover, or at least to slow it down. A lot of people stand to make or lose a lot of money depending on which way they guessed the deal would fall. Maybe your friend on the board had an ax to grind in showing you the letter. Maybe he sent it himself."

"You're awfully suspicious, aren't you?"

"Somebody mentions murder, I get suspicious. Why do you think I'm here?"

"To tell me about the letter, if I didn't already know."

"Of course. But Falzet could have done that on the phone. Or I could. The real reason I'm here is to try to size up your people and see if any of them are behind this."

Dost didn't seem to be surprised. I hadn't expected him to be. You don't work your way up to billionaire status without the ability to see the other guy's angle.

"You seem to be making a big deal out of a little crank letter."

"I've seen thousands of crank letters," I told him. "The Network gets them by the bagful. This one is not typical."

"So it's not typical. It's still a crank letter."

"This one was typed on a laser printer. So we're talking about a relatively well-off crank, or at least one who has access to one of these things and the knowledge of how to use it. It's grammatical and educated in tone."

"Educated people write crank letters."

"*They* don't think so."

"What?"

"Educated people who write threatening letters. They invariably try to make mistakes in grammar or spelling because they feel intelligent people such as themselves would never be suspected of stooping to anonymous letters." I looked at him. "Do I really have to tell you this? No offense, but you must get your share of hate mail."

"I get a couple of people's shares. All right, so it's not your usual crank. What diff——"

"I'm not finished," I told him. "I had my people do some checking. Every member of the board got a copy of this letter. Even Barnard Bass, who lives in Spain, got one. Not a photocopy. That means someone fed the names of *all* the directors into a computer and had separate letters printed up. The envelopes were done on the same printer, so the same someone fed in the addresses, too."

"And that means someone knew the addresses." Dost did not seem happy.

"Right," I said. "Knew them right down to the nine-digit zip code and the number on the office door. That stuff isn't exactly classified information, but it takes some nosing around, and you have to know where to look."

"Where were they mailed from?"

"They were postmarked New York, but that doesn't mean anything. There are mailing services in every town in America these days. A lot of them will get your stuff postmarked from wherever you like."

"I've used them myself," Dost conceded. "When I wanted somebody to think I was somewhere I wasn't."

"Who showed you the letter?"

Dost didn't like it, but he named somebody for me, the president of a Wall Street bank.

"That wasn't so bad, was it?" I smiled.

Dost looked sour, but he hadn't heard anything yet. "Now," I said, "tell me about the family and staff you've got here. Tell me about insanity, treachery, and murder."

5

Bon appétit!
—Julia Child, "The French Chef" (PBS)

Dost left my room with a promise to see that Spot got a water dish and some food. I finished getting dressed. I had never gotten around to asking Dost what the dress code was. I decided on the jacket without the sweater or the tie.

It was time to make a phone call, but I hesitated. There was a phone in the room, and I had the number I wanted to call and the Network's credit card, so that was all right. I just didn't know how things were set up here; how easy it might be for someone to listen in.

I sat on the bed to think. My eyes wandered until I was looking out the window, and then I realized no thought was necessary. I was not fighting my way through that snow and down the goddam mountain just to find a pay phone. Besides, the odds against the letter having anything to do with anyone here were astronomical. I mean, a certain amount of paranoia can be beneficial, but too much is crazy.

I picked up the receiver and dialed a zero, followed by

a number in the 718 area code. Then after the bong, I dialed the Network's credit-card number. A voice came on and thanked me for using AT&T.

I was reflecting that they ought to add plugs on the tape for orthopedists who specialized in sore dialing fingers when Shirley Arnstein answered the phone.

"Matt!" she said. "I'm surprised the phone lines are still up." Shirley was one of the two people in Special Projects I called on for the most important jobs. Shirley had come to the Network from the staff of a congressman who would still be a congressman (and a free man) if he had listened to her advice instead of letting her do all of his work. She's pleasant to look at, though you couldn't call her pretty, and she's very shy about everything but her work. There, she's a tigress. If I told her to find out who put the salt in the sea, she'd come back in a week and tell me. She'd at least have a list of suspects.

"What do you mean?"

"The blizzard! They predicted 'flurries' down here. The whole Northeast is paralyzed. Didn't you see the Network news?"

"No, I watched 'Jeopardy.'"

She clucked her tongue at me. "A fine example *you* set."

Three years ago, she would never have thought of speaking to a vice-president (even me) that way. Part of the change, I'm sure, was Harris Brophy's influence. Harris is the other Special Projects employee I count on. He's small and handsome, with an ever-present air of cynical amusement. Shirley is desperately in love with him, and he's willing to let her be. For Harris, that's large-scale commitment.

"Tell me about the blizzard," I told Shirley.

"Well, here in the city, it's bad enough—traffic snarled, a lot of things canceled—but north of Poughkeepsie, it's a real mess. The highways are all closed, and the airports. Trains are running hours late. Power lines and phone lines are down all over. The Governor has called out the National Guard."

"I'm glad I didn't try to slip out to that pay phone."

"What?"

"Never mind. If telephone lines are down all over, I'd better talk fast." I told Shirley about Gabby Dost's friend, the banker, and asked her to do a thorough but discreet rundown on him as soon as she could.

"I'll get on it first thing in the morning," she said.

"I thought the city was snowed in, too."

"The subway isn't. Not in this part of Brooklyn, at least. And our phone lines are underground, too."

"Call me here as soon as you have anything." I gave her the phone number. "If you can't get through, brief Harris and report to Falzet."

"Falzet?"

"In person. While you weren't looking, the Age of Aquarius got here—harmony and understanding and sympathy and trust and like that. Falzet's like a father to me, now."

"Okay," Shirley said. She sounded dubious. "I hope the phone lines stay up."

I told her I did, too. I hung up, put on my jacket, patted Spot, and went down to join the party.

I met Roxanne on the stairs. She was still grinning like a beauty contestant.

"Hi, Cobb," she said. She almost sang it.

"Hi, Rox. Listen, will you do me a favor?"

"Anything for you, Cobb. You know that."

"Try to look a little more serious, will you?"

"But I'm *happy*. I'm going to get out from under the Network. I'm going to have the monster that destroyed my family behind me at last. And I don't even have to give up being rich!"

She laughed at her own joke. Roxanne Schick drove a Volkswagen Beetle she kept together with Scotch tape, and lived in a two-room, third-floor walk-up. Being rich was not the central fact of her life.

"That's swell," I said, "but if you keep grinning like the proverbial cat that ate the canary, Dost is going to think you think you're putting one over on him. Who knows what would happen then?"

"Okay, okay. I'll be serious. Can't endanger this deal." She made a face. "How's this?"

"I said serious, not hostile."

She started to laugh, tried to stop, and ended up blowing a raspberry of escaping laughter as we entered the main hall.

Norman was a sight to behold. He had traded his flannel shirt for a tux that let bony wrists and ankles show. He was distributing champagne from a silver tray. He swooped down on us. Roxanne took a glass and sipped at it and pronounced it good. I took one, not because I care for champagne, but because if you are carrying a glass around, no one will come along and bother you.

I scanned the room, putting names to faces. Some, of course, I already knew. The big, bluff guy with the red face and white hair was Haskell Freed of the Network Finance Department, and the balding, Ichabod Crane type was his assistant, Ted "Bats" Blefary, with whom I had attended the occasional Yankee game. I had been able to prevail upon the two of them to bring Spot up because Bats is a friend of mine, and because Haskell Freed wants to be president of the Network (or some network) the way Mother Teresa wants to go to Heaven. He is better disposed toward me than toward the other 166 vice-presidents because he knows I'm no competition.

I suspected Haskell, like Falzet, thought I had pull with Roxanne Schick, and tried to stay on my good side for that reason. It would be interesting to see if his attitude changed any after the sale.

We went over to say hello. I thanked them for bringing Spot.

"It was a pleasure," Haskell said. Bats nodded. No trouble at all.

Mrs. Norman came around with hors d'oeuvres: sautéed chicken livers wrapped in bacon and whole-wheat breadsticks dipped in maple syrup, also wrapped in bacon.

"Lord," Haskell said. "I'm trying to lose weight." It didn't stop him from taking one of each.

Didn't stop me, either. "What the hell," I said. "This is the frozen North. We're snowed in. Cholesterol doesn't count in a situation like this. We need *hearty* food. I understand dinner is going to be moose-meat pie and spaghetti."

Roxanne said, "Guys, I think we ought to break up the Network group here and mingle."

We did so. I didn't have to take many steps to do it, either, since I turned around and found myself inches from a blond confection who had to be Aranda Dost.

"Excuse me," I said. I had almost gotten sticky maple stuff on a white satin blouse.

She inspected the site of potential danger. It was a site well worth inspecting. "No harm done, Mr. . . . Cobb.

"That's me," I said.

"No harm done at all. And even if there had been, there wouldn't be anything to worry about. It happens constantly. Gabriel is addicted to those things; if I try to let a gathering go by without serving them, he gets crazy. The liver, too. So unhealthy for him."

I resisted the urge to tell her she meant unhealthful.

She smiled and went on. "Well, I hope everyone enjoys them. I was going to have Mrs. Norman prepare a platter of *crudités*, but apparently the delivery van had to turn back halfway up the mountain. I *knew* we'd have problems with the weather. Already, no one can get in or out."

"The forecast wasn't that bad," I said.

"Oh, no, I mean weeks ago, when the meeting was first scheduled. I asked Gabriel not to bring everyone here. You see . . ." She lowered her eyes and blushed prettily. "I'm psychic."

I looked at her. I always look closely at people who are psychic. Aranda Dost was not as tall as she looked—she was wearing wicked spike heels under trousers that had been cut long to disguise the fact. She wasn't as young as she looked, either. At first glance, seeing the casual style of the abundant golden hair, the makeup and the clothes, you might take her for twenty-five, tops. A closer look showed the fine lines at the corners of the eyes and the mouth, and suddenly we're talking about a woman maybe my age, maybe as much as forty.

I wondered what the idea of the teenager costume was. I remembered Dost's telling me that Aranda was his third wife, and he'd been married to her for fourteen years, a personal best for him. Maybe she was beginning to feel that her term was about up, or could be if she didn't keep her husband from noticing the passage of the years.

Or maybe she was just a bubblehead. "Psychic," after all, is an easy term to throw around. Only good manners kept me from pointing out that predicting a snowstorm on a mountain in upstate New York in the middle of February did not constitute a bold rebuke to the laws of probability.

I thought I was controlling my face, but she read the skepticism there, anyway. Maybe she *was* psychic.

"You don't believe me," she said.

"I'm willing to be convinced."

"Well, the first time I saw Gabriel, I was singing in Chicago. I was a singer, you know."

"Sure," I said. "I've heard some of your records."

"Now, Mr. Cobb. Now I'm not sure if I believe *you*."

I told her the names of a couple cute novelty numbers of the Joni Sommars, Sue Thompson type. Not big hits, but big enough for an oldies fanatic like me to have come across.

"Well, this is a pleasure. Why—ah—where was I?"

"Singing in Chicago."

"That's right. I was singing in a club not far from where I grew up, my first time back to Chicago in years. I had worked so hard at losing my accent—you know I used to have the most *tearbl Shkaago aaxnt*—but there I was, trying not to talk to anybody, and ruin things, when I saw Gabriel in the audience. I didn't know who he was, but I just knew in a flash that this was the man I was going to marry."

I was scheduled to spend four days to a week in this house, with this woman as my hostess, and *I* just knew in a flash that this was a bad time to try to explain to her what constitutes evidence and what doesn't. Instead, I just said, "Fascinating."

She waved a jeweled hand at me. "You still don't believe me. I'll try to make a prediction about you, and we'll see if it comes true."

I smiled. "That sounds fair. I promise not to go out of my way to thwart it. What's the prediction?"

"I have to wait until it comes to me," she said.

Wilberforce and Carol Coretti came downstairs, and the hostess went to greet them. Before she left me, she squeezed my hand and assured me that she had predicted her husband's purchase of the Network, too.

"Yeah," said a voice in my ear. "When he buys it, she can predict all the hit shows, and Gabby'll never have to worry about ratings."

I turned to see a stocky guy in a Western suit, tan, with tasteful white piping. He wore a string tie with a turquoise-and-silver slide and a black Stetson, the whole cowboy number. Except for his boots. Instead of cowboy boots, he was wearing high, lace-up stomp boots. He mentioned that he'd slipped on the stairs and twisted his ankle, and was splinting it with the boots. They looked a lot like the boots that had tormented my feet when I was in the army, but they were brown instead of black.

His eyes were blue and crinkly, and his face was brown and wrinkled but still handsome. I wondered how long he could spend at Rocky Point before that tan started to fade. Despite the Nashville wardrobe, this wasn't the kind of fellow I could imagine using a sun lamp.

He stuck out his hand and told me he was Jack Bromhead. "And you must be Cobb. Gabby's told me a lot about you."

He'd told me something about Jack Bromhead, too. How Jack and he had been partners early on, how when they split up the money Jack had pissed his away, then crawled into a bottle, while Gabby had parlayed his into what the newspapers were pleased to call "the Dost Empire."

When the first frontiers of the Empire began to take shape, Gabby had found his old partner, sobered him up, and made him his right hand. According to Dost, Jack could handle any kind of equipment, solve any problem, and get along with any person or group of people. His only shortcoming, as Dost saw it, was that he didn't have the fire in his belly to become a top businessman.

"He'll still climb an oil rig at the drop of a hat, if you let him, or ride a mankiller if somebody mentions there's one in the stable. Hell, he's my age, too. There's lots safer ways to get thrills."

That description, and the cowboy outfit, had led me to believe that Jack Bromhead would turn out to be another guy who'd picked his way of life to provide himself with a dipstick for his testosterone level. I run into altogether too many guys like that.

It was a pleasant surprise to learn that Jack Bromhead wasn't one of them. I could tell right from the handshake. Bromhead wasn't a crusher. There was a good healthy squeeze, enough to show the strength was there to be called on if needed.

"I don't think Gabby knows a lot about me to tell."

Bromhead laughed. It wasn't quite "haw haw haw," but it was close. "He thinks he does. Besides, lack of information has never stopped Gabby from telling people a lot about anything. Gabby just tells a lot, period."

"I'd noticed that. I like your outfit," I said.

"Thanks a lot."

"It makes me feel a little underdressed, though."

"No, you're fine." He dropped his voice a little. "Actually, I just wore it to annoy Aranda. She hates to be reminded that Gabby and me are Western boys. We've got some money, thanks to Gabby, but we're still Western boys."

Bromhead lifted his hat and smoothed back a bunch of black-and-white curls. "It's not that I don't like her. I've liked all of Gabby's wives. Even the first one, Louise, Barry's mother. I thought I was a mean drunk, but she was the champ. She was a charming gal before she started drinking, though. Mary Ann was fine, but a little flighty. I liked her, though."

"Maybe that's the problem. She doesn't like anybody around with good memories of Gabby's previous wives."

"Nah, it's not that. Louise drank herself to death about five years ago, and Mary Ann lives in Hawaii, and the only contact Gabby ever has with her is when the canceled alimony check comes back.

"It's just something women do, that's all. I guess it's a test to see how much they're loved or something. They've just got to try to force a guy into the position of choosing her or his best friends. Only Gabby and I never let that happen."

"She should have predicted it."

Bromhead lowered his face, then looked up at me under

the brim of his hat. "Yeah. Hey. Your glass is empty. Norman! This man needs some more champagne!"

None of that was true. My glass was still a quarter full, and I had been planning on nursing it along until dinner started. Now I had to gulp what I had and take another, or feel like an asshole by sending Norman away. I took the second glass.

Bromhead was grinning at me. "I'm different from most alcoholics. I really *liked* good liquor. Liked the way it tasted. Now, I stay sober and watch folks who can handle it enjoy it."

"Must take a lot of willpower."

"Not-drinking gets to be a habit, the way drinking was. Like they tell us at AA, one day at a time. What I do is, I keep remembering the bar I was sitting in in Kansas City when Gabby caught up with me, back when. I remember the heat and the smell of sweat and the flies walking on my face that I was too drunk to shoo away. Then I think of what I've got now, the people who call me sir, and want to hold doors for me, and I don't have too much trouble staying away."

I told him I admired him, which was true, and how I doubted that I could do as well in his place, which was also true. He gave it an aw-shucks laugh. This looked like a good opportunity to break away and mingle with the one person I hadn't spoken to yet—Barry Dost, Gabby's only child, currently working for his father as Communications Director, PR man to those of us who are not blood relatives of the boss.

Before I could, though, Gabby Dost made his appearance. "Hell, what's everybody still standing around for? Dinner's ready five minutes ago. If I can't get those donkeys in Phoenix off the phone any sooner, I don't deserve a hot meal. Come on, now, in the dining room. I'll bet Agnes's done herself proud."

She had indeed. This was a spread, this was a *meal*.

Looking at the table, and at Agnes Norman's round face beaming above it, I almost wished I'd spent the day skiing, so I'd have appetite to do it justice. It was the kind of meal you should burn off five or six thousand calories before attempting.

There was a baked ham the approximate size and shape of Roxanne's Volkswagen, and a huge platter of fried chicken. Mashed potatoes, yams, green beans, corn. Cornbread. Crocks of butter and honey.

Aranda Dost was directing us to chairs. Gabby was at the head of the table, Aranda at the foot. There weren't enough women to go around, so Roxanne and Carol Coretti were placed at the centers of the two sides. I wound up between Haskell Freed and Barry Dost. How convenient, I thought. I figured I already knew as much as I needed to about Haskell Freed, so I concentrated on my prospective boss's son.

Barry Dost had his father's features, but there was a softness to him, a blurriness around the edges, that was as unlike the hard-edged Gabby Dost as anything you could imagine. He ate nervously, with little quick bites, as though he were a squirrel afraid some big old tomcat would come and chase him away from his meal.

Not that he was small. I'm six-two, and I didn't have to tilt my head to look him in the eye. When he *would* look me in the eye. Most of the time, he looked at his plate, trying to rivet it to the table with his gaze so the tomcat wouldn't snatch it away from him.

The only time he looked up was when his father spoke. "Attention, please." Gabby Dost was holding a drumstick aloft. "Now you know why I called for a casual meal. When things are casual, house etti-quette overrules formal etti-quette. And etti-quette in this house says there's only one way to eat fried chicken."

He brought the drumstick to his mouth and crunched it loudly. Bats Blefary, Roxanne Schick, Carol Coretti, Jack

Bromhead, and I applauded. Wilberforce wore his usual deadpan. I noticed Wilberforce had a lot of green beans on his plate. He's not a vegetarian, but he might as well be, since the only meat he eats is poached breast of turkey.

Aranda Dost wore a pained smile. The man refused to live up to his income; he insisted on living down to his breeding instead. But what could she do, she loved him, the big lug. I like a facial expression that can speak a whole paragraph, and I almost leaned across the table to tell her so.

And Barry Dost was glaring at me.

"What the hell are *you* looking at?" That's what I wanted to say. That was what I like to call my New York Response. I have to stifle those a lot. Instead, I tried to be friendly.

"Your father seems to be getting a much better press lately," I told him. "That must be your doing."

He looked at me again, not glaring. This time, his big brown eyes were bright. "I've thought so, too," he said. "That he's getting a better press, I mean. I don't know if it's my doing, or if it was just time for a change."

Barry Dost was two years older than I was, but that softness around the edges made him seem younger. He had a mustache that sort of floated on his lip, and didn't help, since it looked as if it had been stuck on him to enable him to portray Kim's father in a high school production of *Bye Bye Birdie*.

Right now he wanted reassurance, so I gave it to him. I told him these things are never spontaneous, that as PR man, excuse me, Communications Director, he must have been doing something right.

"All I did was tell the truth, how much the ordinary people who own stocks in the companies he's bought have prospered. How the companies my father controls are one hundred percent more profitable . . . I mean they've all increased their profits, not that they've all doubled them."

"That's what I thought you meant."

"Charitable donations are way up, too. That was my idea."

He was so enthusiastic about his work, I had to smile. I like to see people enjoy their work the way Jack Bromhead liked to see people enjoy good booze.

Barry saw that smile and cut me off. Cold. Couldn't get a word out of him the rest of the meal. This, I thought, is a person with self-esteem problems.

Dinner broke up, and we went back to the hall for more mill-around. They were standing around in small groups, discussing what they were going to start discussing tomorrow. I heard words like "debenture" and "amortization," and went and stared out the window at the other end of the room, looking at the snow dancing in the ground lights. The snow seemed to have let up some. I wondered how early I could decently go to bed.

I felt a hand on my shoulder. I turned to see Barry Dost. He was glaring at me again.

"I'm not everything my father ever wanted in a son."

I was beginning to get an inkling of what the note was talking about when it mentioned "madness." Not that I was ready to petition a court to get Barry Dost committed. I had just decided I would steer clear of him, if possible. It probably wouldn't be too hard. There must have been fifty rooms in this place.

But in the meantime, here he was, and I had to say something. "Every son feels that way at one time or another, I guess." That ought to mollify him, I thought.

Wrong.

"I don't just feel it, I *know* it. It has been made clear to me ever since I was born. I'm not Gabby Dost's idea of a son."

"Well . . ." I began lamely.

Barry poked a finger in my chest. *"Neither are you!"* he said.

"Stop that," I said.

45

He kept poking. "I've finally got one little thing he respects me for, the image work I've done for him, and it's something I can build on, and I'm not going to lose him now. Especially not to some corporate opportunist like you!"

The hall was big enough so that no one was paying attention to us. Still, I suppose it is a bit much to deck your host's son. That *would* get us noticed. Instead, I just grabbed his finger. I was careful not to twist.

"You want to act like a normal person for five minutes and tell me what the trouble is?" I asked.

His voice was a harsh whisper. *"You just stay away from my father,"* he said. "You stay away from him or I'll kill you."

He pulled his finger loose and ran upstairs. I stood there rubbing my chest for a minute or so, then smiled and said good night to everybody, and went up to my room.

6

We work while you sleep.
—Taystee Bread commercial

Two A.M., maybe a little after. Spot was snoring away in the corner. I was lying there in the dark. I'd given up trying to sleep. I always have trouble sleeping the first night in a strange bed, anyway. Tonight, at least, there were things to think about to pass the time.

For instance, I asked myself, of all the stupid things I had done on behalf of the Network, had there ever been one stupider than this trip? After long and intense consideration, I finally had to answer no.

This is what comes, I told myself, of perceiving Tom Falzet as a human being. You wind up snowed into the middle of nowhere with a bunch of very strange people. I didn't know about treachery or death, but if anybody wanted corroboration of the madness angle, I was willing to cosign the next anonymous note.

It wasn't as if I hadn't been sort of warned. Gabby Dost had told me his wife was "into astrology" and that his son was "sensitive." He hadn't said anything about Jack Bromhead's liking to dress for a private dinner as if he were off to ride the bull at Gilley's, but what the hell.

I decided Dost himself probably wasn't wrapped too tight, since it was obvious that only a maniac would want anything to do with the TV business. I ignored the voice in my skull asking what that said about me.

My job was supposed to be to find out enough to make up my mind whether anybody associated with Dost might have sent the letter to try to break up the merger. Considering the way Barry Dost had reacted over the mere fact (as far as I could tell) that his father refused to spit when my name was mentioned, I was really looking forward to asking him if he knew anything about an attempt to mess up his father's business plans.

I decided to tackle him first tomorrow. Then, when he screamed, and people were asking me why I had to break his finger, I could ask them all at once.

Spot raised his head and got noiselessly to his feet. He ran over to the bed and poked me with his muzzle. I scratched his ears and whispered "good dog." Spot grinned (Samoyeds always grin) and pranced to within five feet of the door of the room, where he crouched, ready to spring.

I groped the floor for the pair of gym shorts I run around in before I go to bed. I had trouble finding them. Spot didn't growl or yip, so there was no immediate emergency I'd have to face naked. I cursed silently, rolled until I could get my head over the edge of the bed, found the shorts. As I put them on, I thought that while the Sloans were paying to have Spot taught to go through this whole routine to detect intruders when you're staying in a strange place (Jane used to travel with a lot of jewelry, you see) they could have trained him to retrieve enough clothing for decency on his way to wake you up.

I heard voices outside, a man and a woman, furtive maybe, but not menacing. I was about to stick my head out to see who it was, since furtiveness was something I was here looking for, when there was a knock on the door.

I opened up a crack and peeked out. Wilberforce stood there fully dressed, down to hat and tie, with his overcoat and gloves on. Behind him stood Carol Coretti. She'd thrown her coat on over a dark blue nightgown. She had untied sneakers on her feet.

"What's this?" I asked. "Making a break for freedom?"

"Don't be a fool, Cobb, we wouldn't get a mile in this snow."

I looked at Carol Coretti, who was laughing only with her eyes. You must get a lot of practice doing that when you work for a boss who has no sense of humor.

I needed a distraction to keep from laughing in Wilberforce's face. Fortunately, he provided it.

"Get dressed, Cobb," he said.

"Where are we going?"

He dropped his voice to a whisper. "Away from these rooms," he said. "Outside."

"Do I get to ask why? And why are we whispering?"

Wilberforce answered both questions at once. "I dislike talking in front of a stranger's electronic equipment, no matter how innocent it seems." He leaned close to me and whispered more quietly. "Miss Coretti has brought me some most disturbing news, and I think you should hear it."

"Outside?"

"Outside," Wilberforce whispered. "For a few moments. Away from the house."

"Okay," I said. "If anybody sees us, we'll just say we decided to make a midnight examination of ski conditions. Give me a minute to get dressed."

When I closed the door, Wilberforce was saying, "*Ski* conditions? The man must be . . ." I never heard what I must be.

I pulled on a sweat suit, then followed Carol Coretti's

lead with sneakers over thermal socks. I came out of my room to find Wilberforce tapping his foot and Carol looking dubious about the whole business.

As far as I could see, we were committing no crime, not even one against hospitality. Where does it say a guest, or three guests, can't slip out to the grounds for a midnight constitutional? This fact did not, however, keep us from shooting furtive looks over our shoulders and whispering to each other to be quiet. I started to feel like a refugee from an old Warner Bros. prison picture.

It was cold outside, a lot colder than it had been when we'd made it from the garage to the main house. The storm had moved through. Now the stars shone bright and hard, through air that was so brittle and still it seemed to snap whenever we moved through it. Area lights reflecting off the snow were as bright as daylight.

I looked at Wilberforce. "As long as we're going to do this, we might as well do it right."

I went down the three broad steps, and soon found myself up to my knees in snow. I was lucky I didn't fall over, because there were actually *six* broad steps under the snow. I considered it. If Wilberforce tried to follow me, he'd be in this thing up to his waist in no time. Carol's legs were bare. This part of the yard was a shallow spot, shielded from some of the snow by the bulk of the detached garage. Anywhere else I tried to take them would be worse.

It was unlikely, despite Wilberforce's paranoia, that the house was bugged. How much more unlikely, then, that the front stoop was bugged. I climbed back up the porch and said, "This will do, I guess."

"Miss Coretti came to me this evening with some disturbing news, Cobb. I thought you should know about it."

"It couldn't wait until morning?"

Carol was apologetic. "I originally wanted to handle it that way," she said, "but when I thought about it, after I went to bed, I realized there was no time in the morning I could be sure of seeing you or Mr. Wilberforce alone. There'd be breakfast, and then we're scheduled for preliminary meetings with Mr. Dost."

"So she came to me," Wilberforce said. He said it as though attractive women were constantly knocking on his bedroom door in the middle of the night. "After I had dressed and admitted her . . ." he said (he wanted to make sure I knew he didn't entertain women in his pajamas), ". . . When I had dressed and admitted her, and heard what she had to say, I decided you must know about it at once."

I could feel the moisture of my breath freezing on my upper lip.

"So she's already told you what she has to tell me."

"She did."

"In your room."

"Yes."

"But now we're standing outside freezing because you're afraid the rooms are bugged."

Carol said, "Oh, my God," and laughed. Wilberforce opened and closed his mouth a couple of times before I took pity on him.

"It's okay," I said. "Even if some mysterious 'they' knows what Carol told you, they won't know what we decided to do about it."

Wilberforce nodded vigorously. "Precisely my th—that is, precisely the right idea. I must admit I didn't think of it myself."

I liked him a lot better for making the admission, with its implied pardon of Carol for Chuckling at the Boss in the First Degree.

"So what's the news?"

Carol blushed prettily. "Mrs. Dost was coming on to me."

"Hold it. *Mrs.* Dost? Aranda?"

Wilberforce was getting impatient. "That's what she said, Cobb."

"Just checking my ears, okay?" I turned to Carol. "Coming on how?"

She was really embarrassed. "You know. Deep gazes. Body language. Touching her tongue to the middle of her upper lip. Double entendre. Leading questions. What do women do when they come on to you?"

"It happens so seldom, I forget. When did this happen?"

"All evening. I tried to stay away from her, when I realized what she was up to. I mean, I was shocked. I mean as a lawyer and a businessperson. Making a pass in the middle of a business conference, for God's sake. But she was always catching my eye. She's very good at that."

"I noticed." Swell, I thought. More insanity. Falzet was going to love my report on this.

"Carol," I said, "think hard. Did you do or say *anything* that might have given Aranda Dost the idea that you're gay?"

She looked at me as if I had suddenly switched to pig latin.

"Come on, it's a simple question. Did you?"

"But I *am*," she said.

Now it was my turn to lose the ability to understand English.

"You are *what*?"

"Gay," she said. "Always have been. It's no secret. I'm not especially butch or anything. But I am definitely gay."

There are a lot of nice people in New York who sleep with members of their own sex, and there is a special etiquette for dealing with them. When a man meets an attractive lesbian, for instance, *under no circumstances* is he allowed to say, "What a waste." So I didn't say it.

I scratched "Ask Carol Coretti for a Date" off my "Things to Do When I Get Back to the City" list, and wondered what to do next.

"I thought you knew," she said. "I thought Special Projects knows everything."

"We only worry about things that could hurt the Network."

"Well, I certainly can't be blackmailed. My parents have known for years."

"Then there's no reason for Special Projects to know. But my original question is unanswered. Did *Aranda* have any reason to think you're gay?"

"What do you mean?"

I was getting exasperated. "I mean, you don't find each other by *radar*, do you? There must be all kinds of subtle things, little signs you look for."

"Cobb," Wilberforce said. "That was outrageous, you will apologize at once."

Carol was smiling. "No apology needed, Matt," she said. "Yes, there are signs and signals, but I swear I wasn't showing any of them. I never do, at work. Besides, I already have a special friend, and I'm not looking."

"I have absolute confidence in Miss Coretti," Wilberforce said. "I have always been able to act on her word as though it were proven fact." He let out an angry little puff of air.

"All right, fine. I'm perfectly willing to take her word for fact. As for acting on it, what should we do?"

"What we should do," Wilberforce said, "is leave."

"You can't even get off the *porch*. I agree with you that beating it has its attractions, but we're stuck. We can either have a confrontation, or play it out. I think we should play it out."

Carol gulped. "You don't mean you want me to—"

"No, of course not. In fact, if she keeps it up and you have to slap her down, do it. I meant, act as though getting this deal worked out is the only thing on our minds."

Wilberforce stuck out his jaw. "I don't like it," he proclaimed.

53

My body heat had melted the snow clinging to my sweatpants, and ice water had soaked my thermal socks. I was freezing.

"I said, 'Act as though.' Pretend. Lie. You're a lawyer, for God's sake, you must be good at it."

"Why Falzet has tolerated you all these years is beyond me," Wilberforce reflected. "I still don't like it. First, Dost's attorneys didn't make it here."

"That could be the weather."

"It still leaves us no one to negotiate with but cronies and family members."

"They are all officers in Dost's corporation," Carol pointed out.

Wilberforce didn't even bother to say "Bah." "Then this shockingly inappropriate advance to Miss Coretti. What can these people be thinking of?"

I breathed on my hands and wished I'd remembered to bring gloves. I remembered Dost's own improper advance to me. I didn't mention it because I knew that if I did, Wilberforce would *never* let me get inside.

"Okay. Now before we become a bunch of statues, anything else?"

Wilberforce shook his head no, but Carol let me down.

"Well," she said, "this is just a feeling . . ."

"Yeah?"

"I don't think Mrs. Dost is gay."

"Why not?"

"She just didn't seem to be. No 'signs.'"

"So she was coming on to you as a joke, or what?"

"No, she meant it. She was . . . excited and curious. But she was afraid. As if she'd never done it before."

"Seems like an unusual time and place to try a new preference, doesn't it?"

"Exactly. That's why it's so weird."

And on that jolly note, we went inside. I went back to my room, took off my wet stuff, then ran some hot water in the tub, sat on the edge and soaked until I could move my toes again.

Then I went to bed and thought about Carol Coretti. Women in New York frequently brown me off by saying, "All the good men in New York are gay or taken." Now I'd run into, and felt attracted to, a woman who was both.

I sighed, turned over, and much to my surprise, went to sleep.

7

. . . Because this is Anything-Can-Happen Day!
—Jimmie Dodd, "The Mickey Mouse Club" (ABC)

I don't know how long it took the screaming to wake me, but it went on for a long time even after I got out of bed.

The noise seemed to be coming from outside the house, from in front of the house, not far from my window. I jumped into my shorts, ran to the window. Tore open the shutters and threw up the sash. My teeth started chattering, but I had gotten a glimpse of what was in front of the house, and I wasn't about to turn away.

I couldn't get any colder than I already was, so I pushed the foot-high pile of snow off the base of the window so I could get a better view. It was about seven o'clock, and the sun had risen high enough to see everything with perfect clarity.

The screaming was indeed coming from the front of the house. Mrs. Norman (who would have thought a nice plump middle-aged lady like that could scream better than Fay Wray?) was standing in my tracks from last night,

57

blasting like a factory whistle. The steamy blasts of vapor that accompanied each scream enhanced the illusion.

Mrs. Norman was also jumping up and down and pointing to something across the snow. I looked where she was pointing and understood why she was screaming.

There was a body out there, maybe forty yards from the house, lying on top of the snow. It wasn't sitting on top of any crust—the top layer has to melt some first before snow can form a crust. It was just sort of *floating* on the soft snow I had sunk into up to my knees just a few hours before. Besides, the figure's arms and legs *had* sunk in the snow.

Unless, I thought, they'd been cut off. There was an awful lot of blood out there. From the waist up, the body was surrounded by a blotchy teardrop of blood, about three feet across at the widest part, tapering to a point two feet beyond the head.

But that wasn't the worst of it. For that whole forty or so yards, from the house in a straight line past that one tall pine tree to the body, there was nothing.

The snow was smooth, white, and unbroken.

Somebody had managed to get over a hundred feet through deep snow, and die messily, *without leaving a mark.*

I went into a trance, then, as that thought got bigger and bigger and uglier and uglier. I wasn't aware of the cold. I wasn't aware of Spot's whimpering beside me, trying to figure out what kind of foolishness I was up to this time. I wasn't even aware of Mrs. Norman's screams.

Then they stopped, and I snapped out of it. Jack Bromhead was out there with his arm around the housekeeper, turning her away from the body and talking earnestly to her. I don't know what he said, but it worked. Mrs. Norman headed inside. Then he started to walk across the snow.

"*Bromhead!*" I yelled.

He stopped in his tracks and turned to look at me.

"Cobb! There's some kind of trouble, I'm going to go see what it is."

"I know what it is," I told him. "Don't track up the snow! You got a camera?"

"Of course!"

"A Polaroid would be nice."

"Got one of those. What's your point?"

"The police are going to want pictures to prove we're not crazy."

"The *police*?"

"Unless somebody fell from a helicopter onto the front lawn, you're damned right the police. Get the camera. And get Dost. He ought to be told about this."

Bromhead looked at me quizzically.

"I know what I'm doing," I lied.

That seemed to help him decide. He started back in. I called to him, "Meet you at the main entrance with the camera."

The first thing I wanted to do was secure that front lawn in case there were any other would-be Saint Bernards in the group. I told Spot to follow me, and ran for the door.

I ran into Roxanne Schick in the hallway. She grabbed my forearms to stop me. The sleeves of her nightgown were soaking-wet and ice cold. "Cobb, there's a *body* in the snow. And blood."

"I know, Rox."

"I heard screaming, so I went to the empty room across the hall from mine to look, and I saw this person spread out in the snow."

"I know, Rox, I'm trying to—"

"Cobb, you have to *do* something!"

"Good idea," I said. It's a lot easier to humor someone in that kind of mood. "I'll get right on it. Come on, Spot."

Mrs. Norman was standing just inside the main door. She screamed again when she saw me. I was insulted until I realized I was still running around clad only in a pair of old red gym shorts. I hadn't brushed my teeth and combed my hair, either.

I told her it was all right, I was no danger to her or anybody, but she wasn't having any. I ignored her for a moment, and did what I'd come down there to do. I told Spot to watch the door. No one would be leaving now, unless he or she considered getting out of the house to be worth a lot of dog bites.

By the time I'd gotten that taken care of, Mrs. Norman had a new tune.

"Help!" she screamed. "Help!"

Just what I needed. I supposed I really couldn't blame her. Her brain had been in the middle of forming the concept "homicidal maniac" when here came a disheveled, mostly naked man running alongside a dog with very sharp teeth.

I knew instinctively that anything I might say or do would just make things worse. I certainly wasn't going to touch her. The last thing I needed was for her to start yelling rape.

I was just about to run away as fast as I'd come—there were things that still had to be done in a hurry—when help arrived.

The screaming woman's husband was briefly in the lead, but he was passed just at the bottom of the stairs by Ralph, our driver. Ralph's appearance startled me for a second, but it shouldn't have. He drove us up here. The car was still here. If we were snowed in, so was he.

If being improperly clad was Mrs. Norman's chief criterion for suspicion, the sight of her rescuers should not have brought her much comfort. Her husband wore pajama bottoms with little beach balls on them and a sleeveless undershirt. Ralph was as bare-chested and bare-footed as I was. He was, however, wearing long pants, the slacks from his chauffeur's uniform. He also had the

hairiest chest I had ever seen. I half expected to see WEL-
COME written out across it.

I started talking before they stopped running. We
finished in a dead heat.

". . . and there are *no footprints*," I concluded. "So no
one should go out there until we've found out all we can."

Norman was puffing, but game. His wife, at least, had
stopped screaming. "What if the poor guy's still alive?"

"Did you look at him?" I asked.

"I did," Ralph said. "From a room across from where
they put me. Froze my arms getting the snow off the
window."

"And?"

"He's dead. If he was alive, he'd still be bleeding."

I turned to Norman, expecting further argument, but to
my surprise he took Ralph's words for gospel. That was
nice.

"Jack Bromhead's off looking for a camera," I said. "And
telling Dost what's happened. But I want to get another
look right away. Help the dog watch the door, all right?"

"What makes you think you're in charge?" Norman
demanded, and if I'd had to answer him, I would have
been stuck. Again, Ralph came to my rescue. He put out a
hand, and said, "Shh, it's all right," and again the butler/
jack-of-all-trades subsided.

I headed back up the stairs, figuring an extra bit of
elevation might show me more. Specifically, I wanted to
see if there was a route to where the body was that would
get you there without leaving tracks in the snow.

I passed some angry and/or bewildered people coming
down the stairs as I went up. Haskell Freed wanted to
know what the meaning of it all was. I would have been
delighted to tell him, but since I didn't have the first
idea, I skipped it. I saw a stocky blond guy I didn't recog-
nize, and stopped for a minute to ask him who the hell he
was. Turned out his name was Cal Gowe, and he was the

other driver, the one who'd taken Freed and Bats Blefary here.

I was pretty well out of gas when I got to the fourth floor. I had been toying with the idea of going all the way up to the top floor to look, but my lungs convinced me to do that only if I couldn't learn anything from here.

I heard sobbing as I reached the top of the stairs, a man's sobbing, hopeless and unashamed. It was coming from the hallway to my right, the way opposite the one that led to where Ralph had told me his room was.

I walked softly down the hallway—it was easy, I was barefoot—until I came to the room at the end of the hall. On the right, facing the front of the house. It had to be the room the cables came into.

The door was open. I stood in the doorway and looked at the electronic equipment that sent the proper TV and voice and telex and fax information to the proper parts of the house, and the panel below the windowsill that held the ends of the wires. There was an icy breeze from the open window.

Barry Dost was leaning over the sill, crying. He was fully dressed, from shiny black oxfords to a dark tweed jacket. Every once in a while, he tried to say "Dad," but it was washed away in a sea of blubbering.

Obviously, Barry Dost knew, or thought he knew, something I didn't. I had had a sinking suspicion that it was Dost out there in the snow ever since I first looked out the window, but I didn't *know*. I wanted to find out why Barry was so sure.

This was going to be tricky. I mean, judging from his little explosion last night, I didn't have to worry about presuming on a friendship. On the other hand, he might hate me too much to tell me anything.

He still didn't even know I was there.

"Barry?" I said softly.

He turned from the window. With his eyes red and

puffy and his nose running like a syrup dispenser, he was no treat to look at.

"What do *you* want?" he said.

"I'd like to know why you think—"

"And why aren't you wearing any *clothes*?"

I made myself a silent promise that the next time I came across an impossibly dead corpse, I would don a goddam tuxedo before I did anything else.

"Too busy to get dressed," I told him.

He sniffed and sneered at the same time, a good trick. "Too busy doing what?"

"Why are you so convinced it's your father out there?" I asked.

"I heard him. I heard him last night. I was in my room down the hall. I heard him walking by. I know his step, and I know his voice. He was talking."

"What was he saying?"

"Why don't you tell me? *You're* the one he was talking to."

"Not me," I said.

"*Liar!*" he screamed. "You're a damned *liar!* He called you by *name!*" His mouth kept moving, but no sound came out. He was approaching complete hysteria. I wondered what the hell I could do for him.

I was still wondering that when he jumped me.

I was too startled to move. He got his hands on my neck and bore me to the floor. What he lacked in technique, he more than made up for in enthusiasm. He kept cheering himself on (or me off) with little cries of "You did it, you bastard, you did it, you did it."

It was time to do something. Like make it possible for me to breathe, for instance. The position we were in, with both my arms free, made it possible for me to do any number of things to make him stop, and fast, but they all involved permanent damage to Barry Dost. I wasn't ready for that. Yet.

Instead, I forced my forearms up inside his, and pried

his hands off me. He felt it happening, and didn't like the idea, but I was too strong for him. He screamed wordlessly as his hands came apart, and I rolled out from under him.

Then he surprised me. He didn't try to jump back on or anything, he just got to his feet, and kicked me hard in the side of the head while I was still rolling.

I tried to get up. I made it as far as my hands and knees, but I had to stop to shake some stars from in front of my eyes. I put my hand to the side of my head, then took it away and looked at it.

No blood, I thought. Hooray.

I made it to my feet, and staggered up against some electronic control panel. The metal was cold and shocked me alert.

He could have killed me, I thought. The goddam overgrown twerp could have killed me. The temple is the thinnest part of the skull. I thanked God, not for the first time, for having given me a thick one.

It occurred to me to peek out of the doorway and see where he was. I looked just in time to see him down at the other end of the corridor, disappearing around the corner to an as yet unknown (by me) part of Rocky Point.

To hell with him for now. Where was he going to go?

But I still wanted a few words with that boy. I could still feel his cold, dry hands on my throat, the cold, dry rough cloth of his jacket against my chest. The toe of his oxford against my skull.

That could all wait. I had to go talk to some people about a corpse.

8

But wait, there's more!
—numerous late-night TV commercials

I stopped at my room on the way downstairs and got dressed. I dressed warmly, because I knew that sooner or later I was going out in that snow. I also tried to phone the cops, but I couldn't raise a dial tone.

Spot was still guarding the door when I got downstairs, but no one in the crowd that had gathered down there was bothering him. They were all looking expectantly at me, as though they were waiting for me to tell them everything was okay and they could go back to bed.

The gang was all here, too. Wilberforce, Carol Coretti, Haskell Freed, Roxanne Schick, and Bats Blefary from the Network; Jack Bromhead and Aranda Dost from G. B. Dost Enterprises; Mr. and Mrs. Norman; and Cal Gowe, and Ralph. The only ones missing were the Dosts, father and son.

"Where's Gabby?" I asked Bromhead.

"Couldn't find him," he said. "Or Barry either. You have any luck?"

"I found Barry. He seems to think it's his father out there in the snow."

Aranda Dost fainted. If it was a fake, it was a good one. Both knees bent to the left and down she went, hard, on the stone floor of the hallway. She was going to have quite a lump on that shapely white elbow. Mrs. Norman gave me a look that would sour milk, then bent to take care of the fallen woman.

Jack Bromhead was in my face. "What the hell's the matter with you, Cobb? Is that the way you tell a woman her husband's lying all bloody and dead not fifty yards away?"

"I didn't say that. I just said that's what her stepson thinks. At least, that's what he says he thinks."

Bromhead backed off a little. "Yeah. Well, I think so too, I guess. It was still a pretty tactless way of going about it."

"I'll apologize when she wakes up. I've just been kicked in the head—see this lump?—and choked, and I'm still a little wrought up, you know?"

"Barry kicked you?" Bromhead's voice said he didn't believe it. "Barry choked you?"

"Yeah, and then took off for parts unknown." I decided to save his accusations for a while. I was none too popular around here as it was.

"I never would have thought he had it in him," Norman said. He sounded proud.

"I didn't either," I said. "That's how he got to me."

"I still don't know what the heck you were doing up there, anyway," Norman said.

"Scouting camera locations," I said, more or less telling the truth. "Do you have the camera, Jack?"

Bromhead held it up for me to see. He didn't hand it to me. "You're getting mighty bossy for a house guest, Cobb."

"Oh, get stuffed," said Roxanne Schick. "Cobb's had experience investigating murders. What have you got? There aren't likely to be any cops here any time soon."

I wanted to kiss her. Not that what she'd said would do any good with the anti-Cobb faction, but it was nice to have the moral support.

Norman answered her. It occurred to me he was pretty mouthy for a servant, but I didn't say anything.

"There's a cop here already," Norman said.

This aroused interest. There was a general chorus of "Where is he?" and "How did he get here?"

"Been here all along. My nephew, Ralph Ingersoll." He pointed to the driver like Ed Sullivan pointing to the Moiseyev Dancers. "He's a deputy sheriff in this county. Got a badge and everything. Show them your badge, Ralph."

Ralph looked as though what he'd like to do was go bury himself in a snow drift. Instead, he reached inside a pocket, took out a leather folder, showed an engraved piece of silvery metal for three seconds, then stuffed it back in his pocket as though he were ashamed of it.

"Okay," I said. "Glad to have someone in charge. Do you have orders for us, Deputy?"

Ralph stood there.

"Look," Jack Bromhead said. "The girl's right. It will be days before anyone can get through here. You're the only law enforcement we're likely to get. Looks like you're in charge, son."

Ralph thought it over for a few seconds, going from face to face as though sizing us all up for the first time. Then he set his lips, nodded slightly, let go a deep breath, and said, "Okay, if I'm in charge, I'll start now. Aunt Agnes, Uncle Fred, you start making breakfast. If you need any help, ask for volunteers. Cobb, you come with me. I want to talk with you in private. The rest of you wait in the room where you had the party last night until breakfast is ready."

Spot said, "Moooort."

I scratched my head. "Ah, my dog ought to be walked and fed."

Norman gave me a sour look. "I'll do it," he said. "I did it last night. And I'll take him out back, so we don't track up that snow you seem all het up about. You just go with Ralph."

I smiled at him. "If it's okay with Deputy Ingersoll, it's okay with me."

Ralph said, "Yeah, sure," and led me up the back stairs to his room.

G. B. Dost didn't let the help live in conditions as palatial as those of his guests, but they weren't living in squalor, either. Ralph's room was clean and modern, and would have cost $175 a night easy if it had been a New York hotel room.

He waved me to a chair and sat on a bed. He looked at me soberly for a few seconds.

Then he said, "Help!"

"Help?"

"I need your help, Mr. Cobb. I'm in this over my head, and I don't know what I'm doing."

"Nobody else seems to think so."

He looked at the ceiling. "That's just Uncle Fred. I scored three touchdowns against Grover Cleveland High in the regionals, and I've been God's gift to the Adirondacks ever since. Please forgive him. He's down on you because he thinks you're stealing my thunder."

"I've had all the thunder I'll ever need," I told him. "I just sort of took charge this morning because I knew what a mess the cops would find when they eventually got here if no one did. Besides, I kind of got to like Dost, in the few hours I knew him."

"I didn't know him. But Uncle Fred liked him a lot. That's another reason he's been in your face."

"It's okay. I didn't know you were a deputy sheriff."

"Yeah. I'm a deputy. A special. Per diem. You know what that means, don't you? I help coordinate snow-plow traffic on county roads. I'd probably be doing that right now, if I wasn't snowed in up here. I help with crowd control at the county fair. I guard the county jail when one of the regular guys is out sick. I've never been to anything like a police academy, and I *sure* don't know anything about murder."

He opened his hands. "But I did take an oath, you know. And whether I like it or not, I guess I *am* responsible around here. At least, I can't figure out any way that I'm not."

I couldn't see any way he wasn't, either. Under the circumstances, the only difference between Ralph and the Attorney General of the United States was that Ralph was here, and Mr. Thornburgh was in Washington. I made sympathetic noises.

"That's why I need your help. I get into New York quite a bit, with the limo-service job. We've got a regular deal with Mr. Dost. Stay over a lot. I read New York papers, and I see the news on TV. I know you've busted some tough cases."

"It's not the way you think," I said. "Those were all cases of having to bust them before they busted me."

Ralph grinned. "Is this really any different?"

"Yeah, it's different. I'm one of your chief suspects."

"Oh, come on."

"Well, I should be. Motive—who knows? Maybe something to do with the business deal we were up here to handle. Do you know about that?"

"Dost was going to buy your company. Buying companies is what he did."

"That'll do for now. Wilberforce or Haskell Freed can give you more details when you talk to them. So can Jack Bromhead.

"Anyway, it could be that for some reason I didn't want him to buy the Network. Or I was having an affair with his wife, and wanted him out of the way. That's something a detective squad could check very easily, but you don't have a detective squad."

"I could understand somebody taking a run at the wife, though."

Ralph was getting younger and younger before my eyes. Right now, he reminded me of a fourteen-year-old suddenly noticing that his best friend's mother was *built*.

"Or, I could just be nuts."

"Anybody could just be nuts," Ralph said.

"Right," I said. "Never forget that. Now. Opportunity. I actually have an alibi for part of the night, but it's no good."

"Why not?"

"First, because my alibi witnesses are two other Network people, and second, I'm going to ruin the alibi myself."

He asked me what I meant. I told him about our little paranoid kaffeeklatsch out there on the front steps. He interrupted only once ("A *lesbian?*"), listening intently, watching my mouth as though actual glimmering pearls of wisdom were dropping from it.

"Why does that ruin your alibi?" he asked when I was done.

"Because the body wasn't *out* there when we were out there. I don't know when Dost died—hell, I'm not even one hundred percent sure it's Dost out there—but his body was not out in the middle of nowhere at three o'clock this morning."

"So whatever happened happened between three and seven, when Aunt Agnes decided she wanted to see how deep the snow was."

"Exactly. And for that, I have no alibi. I'll be surprised if anybody does." It occurred to me that Carol Coretti might be sorry she hadn't taken Aranda Dost up on her offer.

"Anyway," I went on, "that brings us to means. This is the wild card, because I don't know what the hell the means *were*. I mean, the blood patch makes it pretty obvious he's been torn open. Okay, that could be accomplished any number of ways. *But by what means does somebody get a good forty yards from a house without leaving a track?* You figure that one out, and you've gone a good way toward naming the killer."

Ralph's face lit up. "Maybe he walked!"

I shook my head, but there was no stopping him.

"Why not?" he demanded. "Snow isn't wet cement. Maybe he was cut in the house, staggered outside, and collapsed. Then the wind covered up the blood trail and filled in the tracks."

"Ralph." I noticed I was calling him Ralph again instead of Deputy Ingersoll. What the hell. "Ralph," I said. "You're a deputy sheriff. You've seen your share of accidents?"

"Yeah."

"In the wintertime?"

"Of course."

"You've seen blood on snow."

"More than I like to remember."

"Then you know it doesn't work that way. As far as the snow is concerned, blood is no different from hot salt water. It melts down a good long way. Then when it cools off, it congeals. No wind is going to return that, *and* a trail of footprints, to a smooth, undisturbed surface of snow."

Ralph nodded sadly. The death of one's first hypothesis is never easy to take.

"Besides," I went on, "there *was* no wind last night. Even forgetting about any possible blood. *I* stepped into the snow while we were outside, and my tracks are still there, unchanged. *And,*" I added, "there's no blood in the house."

"So we're back to an impossibility again."

"Exactly."

"So the first thing we do is go get that body."

"You keep saying 'we.' It might come back to haunt you. I haven't told you everything yet." I recounted my meeting with Barry Dost in detail.

Ralph shrugged it off. "Barry's always been a little weird, to hear Uncle Fred tell it. I still say the first thing *we* do is get the body."

"All right," I told him. "Don't say I didn't warn you. No. The first thing we do is call the sheriff and let him know what's going on around here. Then we take pictures of the body *in situ* to prove there really are no tracks there."

"*Then* we get the body."

"No, then we have the breakfast you told your aunt to make."

"Breakfast? Why?"

"Because after we get the body and haul it back to the house, I don't think we're going to feel much like eating."

9

Hold it! I think you're going to like this picture!
—Robert Cummings, "The Bob Cummings Show" (CBS)

It was a good agenda. We followed it without a hitch right through to item one.

"The phone's dead," Ralph said. He jiggled the breaker button the way we've all learned to do it from the movies, even though that particular ploy hasn't worked since the inception of automatic dialing.

"Try a number in the house. Try the kitchen. Your aunt should pick up."

He tried. "Uh-uh."

I didn't like that. It wasn't unusual for phone service to go out in the wake of a blizzard. The intercom's going, though, made it seem a lot more likely that someone had been up to mischief.

So all of a sudden, we had a new agenda. I outlined it for Ralph, and he said it sounded like a good idea to him.

We went downstairs and joined the multitude at breakfast. Murder (or whatever) had broken down artificial social barriers. Fred Norman was sitting at the head of the table, in the place occupied by Gabby Dost the night

73

before. Calvin Gowe was filling in for Barry. Aunt Agnes kept bustling back and forth to the kitchen. Uncle Fred pointed to a place that had been saved for Ralph. I sat where I'd sat the night before, and got busy filling my plate. While I did, I looked around at my companions.

They were a quiet bunch, appropriate enough with a death in the house. The only words exchanged were requests to pass the milk or the maple syrup or whatever. Everyone seemed to be eating heartily enough, except for Agnes Norman (who never sat down), Aranda Dost, and Ralph, who, I suspected, was too nervous about his First Case to want to eat.

Roxanne Schick kept giving me questioning looks, but I shook her off. It was show time, and Ralph had the first line.

"I think I have a much better idea of what this gathering was all about," he said. "I'll want to talk to everyone individually, the way I talked to Cobb, here."

Everybody looked at Cobb, there. I tried not to seem guilty. I was too busy storing away bacon and pancakes and home-fried potatoes. I'd passed up the eggs. I don't like eggs.

Their eyes went back to Ralph. This was it.

"Has anyone tried to make a phone call this morning?" he asked. He was a little ominous, but not too bad.

Haskell Freed held up a hand while he swallowed a mouthful of egg. "Yes," he said. "I did. I tried to call the president of the Network when I went up to get dressed. I thought he should know about this."

"What did he say, Haskell?"

"I didn't get through. I supposed the lines were down."

Ralph said, "Well, they must have come back for a while. I was in the middle of talking to the sheriff when the line went out again."

I took a quick look around the table. Did anyone know

he was lying? Aside from a small belch and an "excuse me" from Jack Bromhead, there was no discernible reaction at all. That meant that either Barry Dost was the one who'd screwed up the phones (I wondered again where he was now) or that it's a waste of time trying to find a guilty person by his facial reactions (which I already knew, but can never stop trying) or that the phone's being dead this morning was in fact an accident, and the intercom's being out was some technical side effect I knew nothing about.

I was beginning to think Ralph had come to the wrong person for help.

"We got some things accomplished before we were cut off, though," Ralph went on. "I'm in charge of the case here until they can get an investigator through."

"Any idea how long that's likely to be?" Bats Blefary asked. His tone was casual, but he sure wanted to know.

Ralph shook his head. "No idea."

"The storm is gone," Wilberforce said. His voice wasn't exactly a whine. "You'd think they could lower someone in by helicopter."

"Tricky winds up the side of a mountain," I said. "They'd probably save that for a last resort."

"That's right," Ralph said with an élan that almost made *me* believe he'd been speaking to the sheriff. "Besides, the county's only got one helicopter, and they're using that for emergency rescue work. They've asked the air force at Plattsburgh to help out with that. We're sheltered here, and safe. We've got plenty of food, and a great cook." He smiled at his aunt. "We're going to be pretty far down their list."

"Their list!" Aranda Dost exploded. "My husband is lying out dead in the snow! I don't care about anybody's list!" She got up and trounced out of the room.

Jack Bromhead mopped up some egg yolk with a piece of pancake. "I can see how she feels," he said.

"Me, too," Ralph said. "I just don't know what to do about it. I wanted to tell you people what's going on."

"Oh," Jack said. "Did the sheriff say anything else?"

"Yeah. He named Mr. Cobb, here, a special deputy to help me investigate the case. So if he asks you any questions, answer them. It's official. If you have any problem with that, I guess you can talk to me."

That was it. That was the big lie we'd decided on. I was betting that at least one person knew that for the blatant falsehood it was, but what could he or she do about it?

Ralph patted his mouth with a napkin, a move strictly for show since he hadn't eaten anything, thanked his aunt for a delicious breakfast, and said, "All right, now for those pictures. The camera?"

Jack Bromhead pulled it out from under his chair. "Been carrying it around all morning waiting for Cobb to take it from me."

I took it from him now. I checked the film. There was a new pack inside, ten shots. Bromhead assured me there'd be more available if we needed it. He then volunteered to take backup pictures with his own .35 mm. Nikon with the telephoto lens, and I told him that was a good idea.

So we took pictures. Out the front door, from my window, from the window of the cable room. I had neglected to close that one after my encounter with Barry, so the room was freezing by the time we got there. Bromhead was limping noticibly by then, too, and grunting every few steps from the pain.

"I'm sorry," I said. "I should have thought about your ankle before we got started on this."

"I remembered it. Don't worry about me. I want to do this. Gabby was my friend. I got my arm caught in an oil pump once, damn near tore it off. I worked the hole for three more days before I saw a doctor. For Gabby, I can lace my boot up tighter and keep going." He took off his hat and scratched his head. "I wish you could bring him in out of the snow, though."

"That's the next project," I assured him. "Let's go downstairs."

As we descended, I looked over the Polaroids. Unless you could photograph an hallucination, we still had the same impossible situation on our hands. There was the snow, a twig and a few bits of bark at the base of a pine, the corpse, and the blood. And nothing else.

Downstairs, Ralph told his uncle to bring us to the tackle room.

"Tackle room" was an understatement. What the place looked like was a branch warehouse of L. L. Bean. Fishing equipment filled one wall: rods and reels, creels, waders, and funny hats. The next wall was guns: rifles for everything from jackrabbit to elephant, and all kinds of hunting and target pistols. There were bows and arrows, even a Wrist Rocket slingshot and a can of ball bearings.

"What was he expecting?" I asked. "Apaches?"

Jack Bromhead smiled. "Gabby just didn't like to see a guest ask for something he couldn't provide."

"What's that?" I asked. I was pointing to a broad leather strap with a chain and a metal clip on either end. It looked like a belt for a rhino.

"It's a phone lineman's belt. Came in handy when we were stringing the cable over the mountain. Fastest way up a pine tree. You loop it around, fasten it, lean back, dig in the cleats on your shoes, throw it up a couple of feet, and go on from there."

"Thought so," I said. "Where's the winter stuff?"

He pointed. Ralph had already picked out some insulated suits, ski gloves, and snowshoes for us. He pointed to something standing up in the corner. "We'll take that, too."

It was a toboggan. Good idea. All the things we'd done before going out after the body had been necessary, or at least wise, but I might not have been so assiduous about thinking about them if I hadn't been fighting with a picture of carrying the body to the house slung over my back.

There was nothing else to do, now, so we got togged out and went.

10

. . . And we're gonna go and get it!
—Andy Griffith, "Salvage" (ABC)

We didn't head straight for the body—we walked in a wide arc. I wanted that snow to remain unbroken as long as possible. That was assuming I didn't fall into the damned stuff.

I had never used snowshoes before, and my success on this trip showed a decided lack of natural talent. I had to concentrate on every step. Don't cross the snowshoes. If you do cross the snowshoes, try to remember to lift the one on top first. After a while, by experimenting and watching Ralph, who was hopping along like a white rabbit, I determined that the best way to do it was to walk bowlegged with my toes pointing out, leaving a track like the stitches on a baseball.

Just about the time I got going good, my right snowshoe kicked something hard just below the surface of the snow. I knelt (another circus stunt), brushed away a few inches of snow, and saw a point of black stone. It was one of the pointed rocks that had marked the road leading up to the house. I closed my eyes and tried to picture the curve of the road. If I remembered correctly . . .

Ralph, pulling the toboggan, had reached the body. He stood well clear of it, and of the bloodstain, waiting for me, The Expert, to arrive.

Which I did in about another two minutes. I took the Polaroid from one of the parka's copious pockets and took some pictures. I put them back in the pocket to develop. Then I reached across the body and handed the camera to Ralph, so he could get a few shots from that angle. He put the camera in his pocket, and we looked at each other.

"Wait a minute," I said. "I want to check out a few things." Ralph looked grateful.

I knelt again, less clumsily this time, and felt around under the body. It was just as I had figured. The body was hung up on the points of the stegosaurus plates that made up the low rock wall.

I told Ralph what I'd discovered.

"Yeah," he said. "Well, we knew he must have hit something."

I took my hand out from under. Something sticky glistened on the blue leather of my borrowed glove. I rubbed my hand rapidly in the snow and looked at what I'd left behind. It would be a long time before I ate strawberry jam again.

I was suddenly aware of the cold. My breath-clouds seemed to form ice particles that scoured my face, and the wind cut through the arctic survival gear the way it would have a cotton T-shirt. I wanted to tighten my hood, but I didn't want to bring my hands near my face. I shuddered.

I'd seen death before, and murder, but I'd never been so close to the nuts-and-bolts household details of the job. There had always been cops around to search the body, medical examiners to explain how the death had occurred. All I'd had to do was look, click my tongue, and think about it.

To hell with it, I told myself. Fighting the problem wasn't going to get me anywhere. I took a deep, cold breath.

"Okay," I said. "Let's turn him over."

Ralph walked up, reached across the body to my side, grabbed two handfuls of the ridiculously flimsy jacket the body was wearing and pulled. I got my hands underneath and lifted. It was as easy as moving a piece of wood. I didn't know if it was rigor mortis or the cold, but this was one body that truly lived up to the name "stiff."

The last doubts that this was G. B. Dost were removed as soon as I saw the face. It wore a startled expression, with eyes and mouth both open. Snow clung to his eyebrows. The skin of his face was as white as the snow it had been nestling in.

There was a horrible gash in his abdomen, from about the navel to the sternum. The jacket, a zip-up, spring-weight flannel kind of thing, had kept his insides in place when we'd turned him over, for which I would be eternally grateful to it. There was a huge purple dent in his forehead.

"Let's get him on the toboggan."

We reached under an arm and a leg each and lifted him on. While Ralph covered the body with a sheet and strapped it to the sled, I looked at the depression in the snow.

"If it makes you feel any better, he was dead when he hit the rocks," I said. It sure made *me* feel better. The idea of being alive to feel myself being gutted like a fish with a knife of dull stone was more than I wanted to imagine.

"How can you tell?"

"Two things. The big one, not enough blood. You saw the hole in him. If his heart had been beating when that happened, we wouldn't have been able to get within ten feet of him without stepping in it.

"There's enough blood for my taste," Ralph said.

"No disagreement there. The other thing is the print of his head."

"Yeah?"

"It's all snow, no ice. If he'd lain here breathing at all, the warmth of his breath would have melted some snow. It would have refrozen smooth. It didn't happen."

"Okay. I guess that shot to the head must have been what did it. Fine. Now let's just get him inside."

That's what I wanted to do. Even knowing what was ahead once we got him there, I wanted nothing better than to grab that tow rope and toboggan G. B. Dost back to his fabulous Rocky Point retreat.

"In a minute," I said. "This is a crime scene. What do you do at a crime scene? You look for clues."

"Come on," Ralph said. "There's a body and there's virgin snow. Where could there possibly be a clue?"

"In the blood," I said. There was a depression about the size of a punch bowl, directly below where Dost's wound had been. There was a puddle of half-frozen strawberry jam in it.

"Oh, Jesus," Ralph said.

"My sentiments exactly. Now you know why I wanted you to eat breakfast. Throwing up is never a pleasant experience, but it tends to go easier on you if you have something to throw."

"Just shut up about it, okay?"

"You don't have to look. My gloves are already screwed up."

Ralph took me at my word and turned his back. I plunged my already-gory hand into the puddle. Of course, I told myself, the real way to do this would be bare-handed, so you can feel for things. I told myself to go to hell.

It was like a stunt on some hellish version of "Double Dare." I kept it up fifteen seconds longer than I would have ever believed I could stand it, having found, I thought, nothing.

When I pulled my hand loose, something was stuck to the glove, dangling from between the ring finger and pinky. It looked like a curled red worm, but as the congealing redness dripped away, I could see it was a piece of heavy fishing line. It might have been eight or nine inches long stretched out.

"You brought envelopes, didn't you?" I said.

Ralph said, "Yeah, what have you got?" When I told him, he said, "That's interesting. We'd better check him for a fishing license." He started to laugh. It wasn't the healthiest laugh I'd ever heard.

"Later," I said. "Now let's get the evidence in the envelope and drag the sled to the house."

Ralph sobered instantly. "Sorry. I was just thinking that this is somehow worse than a car crash." He reached in his pocket and brought out a sandwich-sized Ziploc bag. That was even better than an envelope. Ralph had even thought to open it before we left. He squeezed the top to widen the mouth, and I dropped in the thread.

"I've seen highway accidents smeared out over a quarter of a mile of pavement that didn't hit me as badly as this. It bothers me that I can't figure out why."

I shook the line off the glove into the bag. Carefully, Ralph sealed the top. He was very deft, even with heavy gloves on.

"It's because somebody made this happen," I told him. "An accident is tragic. What this is is evil."

"Evil," Ralph said.

"A man is dead in a way that it's impossible for him to be dead. As far as we can see. The person who made this happen is smart, and contemptuous of life. You got a better word?"

If he did, he wasn't offering it. He picked up the loop of rope at the front of the toboggan and looked at me. I grabbed the loop with my clean, left hand, and together we pulled toward the house.

Norman opened the door for us. "That him?" he asked sourly.

No, I thought, these are your Welcome Wagon gifts, how nice to have you in the neighborhood.

"Yeah, Uncle Fred," Ralph said. "Clear the hallway, okay? Clear the path through the whole house. No reason anybody has to see him like this."

"They want to. *I* want to. Pay our respects."

"Later," I said. "Meantime, just clear the way, okay?"

He gave me a dirty look, then looked at Ralph who nodded, gave me another dirty look, *then closed the door in our faces*. I decided that uncle or not, the time was rapidly coming when Fred Norman's ass was going to become intimately acquainted with the toe of my shoe.

While we were waiting, I pulled off my gloves and threw them down on the top step. The wind bit the flesh of my hands like a school of airborne piranhas, but I didn't care. I was just glad to see that the leather and Scotchguard had held, and my hands were clean.

The door opened. Norman held it for us while Ralph and I took the front and back of the toboggan like a stretcher and carried it through the house. This was a calculated risk. Fortunately, our passenger did not drip. We carried him through the house, around the back stairs, through the kitchen, out the back door, across a patch of snow that had the prints of a dog's paws in it, into a roomy toolshed out back.

The toolshed had been picked because it was the best place to preserve the body until someone who knew what the hell he was doing could see it. It was cold, so it wouldn't spoil, and it sealed well against the predations of wild animals.

Uncle Fred Norman may have been a royal pain, but he could follow instructions. The big worktable in the shed had been cleared and covered with a clean white sheet. There were a stack of sheets, several rolls of paper towels, and a new package of plastic leaf bags close at hand. A bare electric light directly above the table illuminated the shed.

We put the toboggan down on the floor, then lifted Dost to the table. Ralph started shifting around on his feet like a man who has just remembered an appointment.

"Well," he said, "I'll leave you to do what you have to do—"

I looked at him. "Are you an idiot or what?" I asked him. "Ralph, old pal, let me remind you that we did not in fact talk to the sheriff. Remember? He did *not* make me a special deputy. I am a *suspect* in this case. Okay, these are unusual circumstances, I have some experience as an MP and with the stuff I've done for the Network, so you're letting me help out. But believe me, leaving a suspect alone with the corpse is a good way to get yourself in deep, deep trouble."

Ralph sighed with resignation. "So I stay," he said.

"You stay, you help, and you take pictures."

Now he pulled off his own gloves and took out the camera. "Let's get it over with," he said.

This part of the process was every bit as grisly as what had gone on outside, but at least it was more comfortable. Uncle Fred had set a kerosene heater going for us; in a little while, we could work in rolled-up shirt sleeves. There was a sink, too, with running water that approached warmth.

The first thing to do was to get Dost's clothes off. We had to cut some of them off him. We were careful not to cut along seams. Things accumulate in the seams of clothing, and a good lab could perhaps learn things from the small particles they might find there. The clothes went into one of the leaf bags. I was going to put a tie band on it, but

Ralph waved me off, took the bag, and tied three tight knots in the thing—his own special brand.

"This way, the only way somebody's going to get at these clothes is to rip the bag," he said. "No secret peeks."

"Good idea," I said.

"Not bad for an idiot, at least."

"I'm sorry," I said. "That was just built-up tension. This isn't my favorite way to spend a winter morning."

Ralph cracked up. He apparently had a lot of tension built up, too. Pretty soon, I joined him.

"Shh," I said, still laughing. "They'll hear us."

"So who's the deputy sheriff around here? Who's in charge?"

"We sound like a couple of ghouls."

Ralph said, "Yeah," then giggled a few times, then sobered. "Ghouls. Let them go do what we just did. Especially what you just did. Yeesh. I thought I was tough."

"Tough has nothing to do with it," I told him.

Ralph asked me what I meant, but I didn't answer him.

I threw another paper towel into the nearly filled leaf bag and said, "I think that's about as clean as we're going to get him."

"What about the—"

"I'm not going to touch that. Leave it for the medical examiner, when we re-establish contact with civilization."

"Good."

"Let's turn him over." It only took a second. We were getting good at this.

Ralph took some pictures. "Get that area around his shoulders," I said. "Make sure you get those marks."

There were bruises, recent ones, on Dost's back, two lines running from the deltoids close to his neck in straight diagonals to his armpits.

"What the hell are those?" Ralph asked. "They're not like the other stuff, the post-mortem . . ."

"Dependent lividity. That's the blood pooling in the

parts of his body lying lowest after he was dead." I frowned. "No, this isn't that."

"I can't think of a way somebody would get bruises like that," Ralph said.

"Unless he was in the habit of beating himself with a stick."

Ralph said he doubted it. I agreed.

It was time to turn Dost back over. Ralph asked me how I knew all this stuff. I told him that I had been a very enthusiastic MP with a very enthusiastic superior officer. That was true. What I didn't tell him was that I'd picked up a lot of stuff hanging around mystery writers, too.

"Okay," I said. "Let's cover him up."

We spread a sheet over the remains of G. B. Dost, late billionaire, turned off the kerosene heater, and went back to the house.

The whole gang was waiting for us as we stepped into the kitchen. Almost the whole gang.

"Hello," I said. "Any sign of Barry?"

"Nobody will find him before he wants to be found," Jack Bromhead said.

Aranda Dost had returned to the fold. I was glad. I should never have let her run away on her own like that. Her eyes were red and puffy, but she was not now crying. "What took you so long?" she demanded. "What have you been doing out there?"

"Trying to find out as much as we can without messing up the evidence for the experts. When they finally get here."

"Why take the chance?" It was Haskell Freed in his best clubroom voice. The one that said, "Yes, I'm challenging you, but it's no big deal, let's have a drink."

"Yes," Wilberforce chimed in. "You've done everything decency could demand. Why don't you just leave well enough alone until the experts get here?"

I looked at him. I looked at all of them.

"Are you serious?" No answer. "Do you people think Ralph and I spent the morning waltzing with a corpse because we *liked* it? Because of an ego thing?"

Roxanne, God bless her, gave her head a little shake. The rest of them, Dost people and Network people alike, glared at us.

"Listen, assholes," I said. "Get a firm hold on the following fact: *We are trapped in this house with a killer.* A killer who can do things we can't understand. A killer who has, under our noses, bumped off one of the most powerful men in the world. Got that so far?"

Throats were cleared, but I didn't give anybody a chance to say anything.

"What makes any of you think this guy is finished? We might not have *time* to leave it for the experts. There might not be anybody left for the experts to talk to."

Fred Norman's face was red. "Damn you, Cobb, you're frightening the women."

Ralph said, "Shut up, Uncle Fred," and I wanted to kiss him.

"Only the women?" I said. "That's too bad. I wish we all were as scared as I am right now. I suggest from now on you barricade your doors when you're alone in your rooms, and that none of us ever goes anywhere except in groups of three or more."

I paused for a second, and listened to myself. I realized with a shock that unless Barry Dost had offed his old man, I was undoubtedly addressing the killer. Who was undoubtedly eating this up with a spoon.

"Be careful," I said.

Ralph told everyone to hold himself available for questioning this afternoon, and the gang broke up. In groups of three or more.

11

. . . And find the correct answer hidden
somewhere in the puzzle.
—Jack Narz, "Now You See It" (CBS)

Ralph and I spent the rest of the morning exploring the house. Roxanne tagged along, immune to the hundreds of hints I threw her way. When I flat out told her to beat it, she told me I'd said groups of *three*, and she didn't think I'd be the type to make a rule I wasn't prepared to follow myself.

Deputy Ingersoll could have run her off by virtue of his badge, but he was useless. He just grinned and said, "She's got you there."

I turned to Roxanne. "Okay," I said. "But you keep your mouth shut tight about anything we see or say, or I swear to God, I'll take you over my knee and spank you."

Roxanne made her eyes wide and put her finger in her mouth. "Promise?" she breathed.

"I want *you* to promise."

"All you have to do is ask me, Cobb. You should know that by now. I promise to keep my mouth shut."

Ralph had the master key in his pocket and a lot of

enthusiasm for the project. I could understand that. By keeping busy, we wouldn't give ourselves time to dwell on our little Doctor Frankenstein and Igor act from this morning.

In the end, I'm not sure Ralph didn't get the worst of it, since it had fallen to him to play funeral director and usher to those who wanted to see into the shed to view the remains. I stayed in the kitchen and watched them as they came back out. Aranda Dost came back in tears. Ralph practically had to carry her. I don't think either of them minded. Jack Bromhead had his jaw clenched. Agnes Norman kept shaking her head, nonono, muttering "What an awful thing," over and over. Uncle Fred looked twenty years older. He seemed absolutely stricken, as though he'd lost a brother or a son.

And Wilberforce had come back from looking at Dost's body looking, as usual, as if *he* had died and been embalmed already. I put Wilberforce high on the list for afternoon questions.

We decided to start in the basement and work our way up. We were looking for two things: (1) Barry Dost, and (2) anything else that might be of use.

There was a swimming pool in the basement. It wasn't Olympic-sized, but it was bigger than what most people have in their backyards. There was a three-meter diving board at one end. The room was steamy, and there was such a smell of chlorine in the air I was afraid my eyebrows were going to turn white.

We walked around the pool, looking in all the corners. The rest of the place was slick, light-blue tiles and light fixtures. You couldn't hide a guilty thought in there.

Roxanne said, "Damn."

"What's wrong?" I asked.

"Look at this great pool. Swimming and skiing, and I'm not going to get to do either one."

"Maybe you could ski down the mountain and get us some help."

"Very funny. Unfortunately, all the trails run from the top of the mountain to here. I couldn't even get to the lift out there without messing up your precious snow."

"So why can't you swim?"

"'Groups of three or more,' remember? What am I supposed to do? 'Mrs. Dost, is it okay if I organize a pool party? Got any hot dogs and daiquiri mix?'"

"She's got you there, too," Ralph said.

"You be quiet," I told him. I turned to Roxanne. "Did you tag along here to help or to complain?"

"I don't see why I can't do both," she said.

"As a favor to me, then, try to keep the mix about seventy–thirty in favor of help, okay?"

"Sure, Cobb."

"Good." We searched the shower room, the changing rooms, found nothing. We tried the rest of the cellar—storage rooms, et cetera. Still no luck.

On the ground floor, we ran into nothing but resentful looks from the Normans and the other guests.

Until we went to the gun room. I took a Ziploc bag out of my pocket, and headed for the fishing tackle.

Roxanne pointed to the bag. "What's that?" she asked.

"Little piece of fishline," I said.

"What's the brown stuff?"

I looked at her.

She gulped. "Oh," she said. "What are you going to do now?"

"I'm going to try to find out exactly what kind of line it is, and where it came from, so I can figure out what the hell it was doing out there with Dost."

"Maybe that thing he was wearing was his fishing jacket or something."

I frowned. "God, I never thought of that. You're probably right. Still, as long as we're here, let's take a look."

It didn't take long. The narrow drawers below the racks, like specimen drawers in an entomology lab, bore convenient labels like DRY FLIES or .22 LONG AMMO, but they were all locked. I decided to get the key later, if I needed it. Instead, I looked at the rods racked up against the wall.

And there it was, on the reel of a long, thick surf-casting rod: messy tangle where someone had too hastily pulled some line free and cut or broke it clumsily. I supposed someone could have broken it. Not easily, though; it was good strong stuff.

Of course, why someone would keep a surf-casting rod at a mountain lodge four hundred miles from the ocean in the first place was beyond me. It was something we'd have to ask Jack Bromhead.

After that, we went upstairs. This is where things got tricky. I was dead serious about spotting the killer before he expanded his scope. On the other hand, if we did spot the bastard, I wanted the DA up here to be able to put him away. I didn't want to go tainting any evidence.

But warrant or no warrant, we were going to toss the rooms.

As far as I could figure out, the position was this: Ralph had the master key with Aranda Dost's knowledge and consent. Therefore, her room and the rooms of everybody who lived here on a regular basis were fair game. The guests' rooms would take a warrant to search legally, unless we had the occupant's permission to look.

Without permission, nothing we found could be used in court as evidence. This was definitely true for Ralph, and, I suspected, equally true for me and Roxanne. No, the sheriff hadn't really made me a deputy, but by virtue of my "assisting" Ralph on the case, I became a "police agent." Especially if he let me in with that master key.

What a mess. I should have gone to law school the way my father wanted me to. Wilberforce and Carol Coretti were both lawyers, of course, but not the right kind.

Besides, even if they had been, they were still suspects. I would have been silly to follow their advice under the best of circumstances. Even worse, they might have told me there was absolutely no legal way I could look in those rooms.

And I *was* going to look in those rooms. The Supreme Court is very august and wise and all that, but I guarantee you, their decisions would be a little different if, instead of sitting safe in a marble edifice in Washington, they had to hold their deliberations snowed in with a homicidal maniac.

We started with the rooms not technically off limits. The Normans had done their best to turn their quarters in a mansion into a split-level ranch in suburbia. One of them was addicted to milk-glass cherubs and paintings on black velvet of little kids with Big Sad Eyes. I was beginning to understand Fred Norman better. If I lived surrounded by that kind of crap, I'd have to take it out on somebody, too.

Jack Bromhead's third-floor room revealed nothing except the fact that the man had resisted at least one of Aranda's decorating ideas. His bed was an antique, but it was an antique boardinghouse monstrosity. The thing was all iron: legs, headboard, and built-in, open bedspring. There must have been a ton of metal in it.

Aranda and Dost had adjoining rooms. Aranda had astrological charts, tarot cards, yarrow sticks, and the complete works of Shirley MacLaine. She had her zodiac sign embossed in gold on her diaphragm case.

I showed it to Roxanne. "What sign is this?"

"Virgo."

"I thought so. On a diaphragm case. The sad thing is, she probably doesn't even suspect that's funny." Dost's room was exactly like mine; it looked as though someone had first parked there last night. It was depressing that a man with G. B. Dost's money and power should have made little impression on his surroundings.

We pressed on. Ralph, Cal Gowe, nothing. We tried all the unoccupied rooms, just in case Barry Dost was cowering under a bed somewhere, but still nothing.

Now for the guests. My room first, to use the bathroom, and to check in with Spot. He was delighted to have a chance to play with Roxanne. Then to the other rooms. Wilberforce's room had all the personality of its occupant, so we were out of there in five seconds. Haskell Freed had made his place a pigsty; clothes scattered everywhere, scraps of paper lying around. I picked up the paper. Each piece was covered with figures, including one by the phone that had a telephone number on it. It *wasn't* the Network's number. I memorized Haskell's number and put the papers back more or less where I'd gotten them.

Carol Coretti's room was next. Roxanne had joined us by now, with Spot in tow.

"What the hell is this?" I asked. "The Wizard of Oz? Every time I turn around, there's more of us."

"Oh, be quiet," Roxanne said. "Spot can sniff out Barry Dost for you."

"Spot is lucky he can sniff out his dinner dish. He was bred to be a sled dog, not a bloodhound."

Roxanne changed the subject. "Whose room is this, Carol's? Bet you don't find a diaphragm in here."

"Droll," I said. "How did you know?"

"*Ha!*" Roxanne shouted. "You mean she *is?*"

"She got you again, Cobb," Ralph said.

"Thanks, Deputy Ingersoll, I might not have noticed." I turned to Roxanne. "Will you stop hooting, please? Or would you rather set off a skyrocket announcing: YOUR ROOMS ARE BEING SEARCHED?"

Roxanne shook her head in wonder at herself. "Wow. What instincts the kid has."

I ignored her, then gave the room a quick look. I found no diaphragm. There was nothing of any relevance to the case, either. The only thing worth looking at was a silver-framed photograph of Carol Coretti with her arm around a plump little blonde.

Roxanne was at my side. "The competition, huh?"

"Rox, knock it off, okay?"

"I saw you mooning over her all the way up in the car."

"I do not moon. In any sense of the word."

"Hey, I knew you when Monica was still around, so you can forget that line."

I smiled in spite of myself. "I didn't say I've *never* mooned."

"That's one for Cobb," Ralph said. "We about done here?"

"Yeah," I said, "let's press on."

I could detail what we found in Bats Blefary's room and all the rest, but it wouldn't do you any more good than it did us.

We did discover a few things. Gabby Dost had been exaggerating slightly when he'd said the place was finished. Only five or six rooms besides the one his family and guests were occupying came up to the standard set by my room. The rest were furnished, but not decorated. The TVs were in place, but were still on wheeled stands instead of ensconced in custom-made mahogany. They were plugged in, but not hooked up to cable or VCR, or even house antennae.

We discovered what had happened to the telephone service, too. The switching console that had controlled the separate lines to the separate rooms, the telex, the fax machine, and the rest of the voice communications system was in a closet backstairs on the third floor. We noticed it especially because the lock had been forced.

The console had been wrecked beyond repair. It looked as if someone had hit it with an ax, then stomped on the pieces.

"Somebody knows we lied," Ralph said.

"Worse than that. Somebody wanted to make sure we couldn't call for help."

Roxanne was still catching up. "How could you possibly have gotten through to the sheriff with that thing all broken—ohh. Somebody knows you lied. You mean me?"

"In addition to you. The person who did this knows we never got through to the sheriff. Now you know why I wanted you to promise to keep your mouth shut."

"Can't you get in trouble doing what you're doing? Impersonating an officer or something?"

"That's the least of our worries," I said.

"Well," Ralph said. "At least we know this guy is serious."

"The dead body on the rocks wasn't serious enough for you?" I demanded.

"I mean *really* serious," Ralph said.

"He means," Roxanne said, "a really serious threat to the rest of us."

"I know what he means," I said. "Come on, let's finish this up." So we did. We looked at a million empty rooms. Well, it seemed like a million. I was getting a headache. The headache reminded me to look in the room in which my pal Barry had tried to kick my head in. Nothing had changed, except now the sun coming through the big square of glass had heated the place up so that it was quite warm. Of course, I had clothes on now, too.

We saved the best for last—Barry's room.

And found nothing. Except for the fact that Barry had imposed some of his personal taste on his stepmother's decorating. There were three walls of bookshelves in Barry's room. One held nothing but books on public relations, one was college texts on clinical psychology, and the third was strictly sword and sorcery novels. There was a case of videotapes—horror movies and cartoons.

"*Chacun à son goût,*" Roxanne said. "That's French for 'Everyone to his own taste.'"

96

"Excelsior," I replied. "That's Latin for 'Let's look in the attic.'"

There was nothing in the attic, either.

What I needed was a couple of Advil and a nice long nap.

"Let's go ask people questions," I said.

12

I'll give it a seventy-five, but I wouldn't buy it.
—Numerous teenagers, "American Bandstand" (ABC)

We set up shop in the library. There were comfortable leather chairs and a bar, in case anyone needed his tongue oiled.

We questioned Calvin Gowe first. He hadn't seen or heard anything. *(I'm a sound sleeper, you know?)* He had formed no opinion of the people he found himself snowed in with. *(I mind my own business, you know?)* Ralph, who worked with the guy pretty frequently, told me that sounded like a fairly accurate summary of Gowe's capabilities, so we put him to work watching the door. "We don't want anybody listening at keyholes," Ralph explained.

Cal didn't care. He did, however, exact his price. "I didn't know you was a deputy sheriff," he told Ralph. He sounded hurt. "You see, I got this outstanding dangerous-lane-change ticket, I wonder if you could maybe help me out. . . ."

I told him Ralph would do what he could, which got me a smile from Gowe and a dirty look from Ralph. But it got us a doorman. I told him to send the Normans in first.

I let Ralph ask all the questions, in the interests of peace. He was pretty good at it, too. He didn't take anything at face value, just because the questionees were close relatives. Not that it did any good. They hadn't seen or heard anything. They had no idea how Mr. Dost's body crossed the snow without marking it. They wouldn't dream of accusing anybody here of such a crime. No, they couldn't tell us where to look for Barry Dost.

"There are so many *rooms*," Aunt Agnes said.

"He could just stay ahead of a search, and slip back into a place you've already been, you see," Uncle Fred said.

"He always has been high-strung," Aunt Agnes said. "And he was doing so well, lately, too. And then this had to happen." At which point husband and wife turned at me and offered me identical expressions of distaste.

I spoke for the first time since they'd been in the room. "Now wait just a darned minute here. You two have been on my case since this morning. Do you sincerely think I killed your boss? Or do I just have BO or something?"

"The way you talk," Fred Norman said. I guessed I wasn't supposed to say "BO" in front of a lady. I apologized.

"You don't mean it. You come here all city-wise, slick as a Teflon griddle. And when trouble comes up, you just take over, running around half-naked, bossing us poor, dumb hicks around, ignoring the real lawman in your midst."

"Mr. Dost never treated us like that." Aunt Agnes sniffed.

"Mr. Dost wasn't City," Uncle Fred explained. Judging by his face and voice when he said it, I decided "City" was synonymous with "pond scum."

Uncle Fred wasn't done. He went on about how I might have fooled the sheriff, and even poor Ralph, but I didn't fool him.

"There was never any trouble until Mr. Dost took up

with you Network people," Norman said ominously. He stared at me, waiting for me to squirm under the crushing weight of his logic.

I just looked at him. Him and his wife. I couldn't believe it. They were *rubes*. Backwater American *rubes*. I'd thought the breed was extinct, but no. Here they were in the flesh, a couple so intimidated by city people, they think every word and every gesture is intended to offend. I'd read about them, but I'd never expected to run across any in this day and age. I sure hope I never meet any more.

I turned to Aunt Agnes. "We'll have our lunch in here," I told her. "Sandwiches will be fine. You may go, now." Might as well be hanged for a sheep as for a lamb, I thought.

They sniffed their way out of there. Ralph turned to me and shrugged. I grinned at him, said, "What the hell," and told Calvin to send in the next victim.

We spent the better part of six hours questioning people, and I could show you the big pile of negatives we accumulated, but it wouldn't do you any more good that it did us. In fact, less, because at least we got to eat ham sandwiches on Aunt Agnes's homemade bread while we accumulated them, which was some minor consolation.

Suffice it to say nobody saw, nobody heard, nobody had any ideas. As for the rest of what was said, I'll just give you the highlights.

Haskell Freed came in smiling, as though he were about to close a deal. He pulled a cigar out of his pocket, started to unscrew the tube, then looked up from his chair and said, "Oh, I'm sorry. Is it okay if I . . ." He tilted his head toward the cigar.

We told him to go ahead, and he beamed at us through clouds of smoke as he got the thing going. He was acting like a man lounging in the park humoring a couple of kids who want to play cops and robbers.

Fine, I thought. I hope he has fun.

"Haskell," I said, "I'd like to take advantage of some of your financial expertise. Something occurred to me, and I wanted to check it out with you to see if it's feasible."

"Of course," he said. He leaned back and took a puff.

"Since Dost announced he wanted to buy the Network, Network stock has been rising, hasn't it?"

"Through the roof. Do you own some?"

"A little. It's impossible to be a vice-president at the Network without accumulating *some* stock. Isn't that right? I mean, you've been a vice-president a lot longer than I have, you must have a lot more stock."

He shrugged. "A fairly significant amount," he admitted. "Nowhere near what Roxanne Schick has, for example. Of course, that came from her family."

"Of course," I said. "Now, it occurs to me that if knowledge or even rumors of this little gathering had gotten out before we came up here, the stock would be peaking just about now, wouldn't it?"

"It would have," Haskell said. "But it won't for long."

"Why not?" Ralph asked.

"Because Dost is dead. Dost was the magic name. Even if the merger were to go through, which, believe me, it won't, the public won't care, since it won't be Dost who's heading up the combined enterprise."

"So without Dost, demand will go down, and the price will go down."

"Down the toilet," Haskell conceded sadly. "I've probably lost paper profits of two million dollars today. Or I will, as soon as the word gets out. I must say, Deputy . . . Ingersoll?" Ralph nodded. "I must say that the sheriff's department is remarkably discreet. The word of Dost's death has yet to leak out."

"How do you know that?" Ralph asked.

"Because although the phones seem to be out, the cable TV is fine, and I've been watching the ticker on the Financial News Network. Network stock is still going up, and all of Dost's other companies—NorAmBake, Dost Tool Company, all the rest—are doing just about as expected. If the word got out, they'd all be dropping drastically."

"But what if somebody knew right now Dost was dead? This would be a great time to sell, wouldn't it? You could make a couple of million in profits. When the stock bottomed out, you could buy it back and have a much bigger block of stock than you had before without having to dip into your pocket for a penny in cash, except for broker's fees."

"That's illegal, Cobb," Haskell had had enough of the game, but us kids weren't going to let him go.

"Murder, too," I said. "We're obviously theorizing about a sick individual here. Somebody, say, bitter over having twice been passed over for the presidency of the Network, facing the fact that if somebody like Dost bought the company, the parade would really have passed him by."

Haskell's face began to get red. "By God, I don't like this, Cobb."

I was amiable. "You don't have to like it, just listen to it. Yes, I *am* talking about you, Haskell. No Dost, no merger. *And* a chance to accumulate enough devalued Network stock to force a change at the top.

"You weren't trying to call Falzet earlier, were you? You were trying to call your broker and tell him to start selling."

I'd caught him with that one in the middle of a puff. It can't be good for you to gasp down half a cigar in one breath, and Haskell Freed's face went from bright red to sea-green in a second. He coughed for about five minutes. Ralph got him a drink of water, which he downed eagerly. Half of it wound up on the burgundy sweater that went so beautifully with his white hair.

Haskell sank back to his chair and caught his breath.

"You okay now?" I asked.

He was wet, and his eyes were teary, but he drew himself up and became formidable. "You've accused me of murder, Cobb. I don't like it. And I won't forget it."

"Your broker just better have the right answers to some questions when we can finally get word out of here, that's all."

"I can't believe this. Do you really think that I killed Dost?"

I was stern. "Do you want the truth?"

"Of course I want the truth."

"No, I don't."

If Ralph had had a cigar, he would have been choking on it. "You *don't?*"

"Haskell's no fool. If he were going to set this up, he wouldn't depend on being able to get a message out to his broker. Suppose something roused the house, and his moves were being watched, the way they are now? He wouldn't be able to count on the word not getting out for enough time for him to take his profits without being too obvious about it. He wouldn't have lied about whom he'd tried to call, and he wouldn't have nearly choked to death when we confronted him with the lie. He also wouldn't have admitted trying to make a call in the first place."

I turned to Haskell. "What you would have done was to have sold your stock *already,* before you even came up here. You'd give up a few dollars for the security. Then you wouldn't have to worry about how quickly word of Dost's death got out. The sooner the prices dropped, the sooner you could buy back in. You could do that openly. Hell, as far as the Network would be concerned, you'd be a hero. It would help you in your power grab."

Haskell reached to his breast pocket for a handkerchief to wipe his brow, but we were being informal today. Haskell's sweater had no breast pocket, and therefore, no handkerchief. Ralph handed him a cocktail napkin.

Haskell took it without a word and blotted himself. All

the while, he gave me a stare that Fred Norman would have been delighted to add to his repertoire.

"Why did you do this, Cobb?" he asked. "I've just passed the worst twenty minutes of my life. Why? Did I do something to you?"

"You *lied* to me. This morning at breakfast. We're rubbing elbows with a killer, and all you can think of is trying to line your pockets. And lie about it."

"I just wanted to avoid . . . You asked if the phone was working. I was just trying to *help* without . . ."

"I know what you were trying to do, and I know what you were trying to avoid. Listen, Haskell. Trying to call your broker was tricky. Lying about it was tricky. And the one and only thing we can say about the person who killed Dost is what a tricky son of a bitch he is. Now. You're not going to be tricky to Deputy Ingersoll and me anymore, are you?"

"No," Freed said. He narrowed his eyes at me. "No, I'm not. Are you done with me, now?"

"Unless we think of something else."

Freed stood up. "Fine," he said. "We'll talk more about this when we get back to the city, Cobb." He looked at me, probably to see if I was going to tremble. When I didn't, he left.

Bats Blefary was next. He came in, took a sniff, and started trying to wave smoke away. He sat in the leather chair without waiting to be asked.

"Whew. Haskell and his cigars. I have to put up with them at the office, of course, but I thought he was going to gas me and Spot dead in the car on the way up here. What can I tell you? I'm not sure how I can be of help, but fire away."

"Okay," I said. "Here's one. Why the hell are you so jaunty, Bats?"

He threw one skinny leg over the arm of his chair. "Look. A paid vacation in the mountains. That was good

105

enough before, when there was work to do—now, I'll just let the money pile up back home, and wait here until spring."

Ralph was taking a dislike to the man. "Doesn't Mr. Dost's death bother you?"

Bats put his leg down on the floor and looked surprised at himself. "Yes. Of course it bothers me. I mean, I'm sorry for anybody who dies hurting. But you know, it's easy to forget about him as a person. For weeks he's been this secret savior of the Network. The way we talked about him in planning sessions made him seem like somebody from another planet—'*Dost*' can give us this, '*Dost*' will want that, the '*Dost people*' will insist on something else. Am I making any sense?"

"A little," Ralph conceded. "You're trying to convince yourself not to be scared."

"Scared?" Bats rolled his eyes up as if to look inside his own skull. "No, I don't think I'm scared."

"Doesn't the prospect of being trapped with a murderer bother you?" I asked.

"Not really. Why should a murderer be after me? I just work for the Network. I don't even own any stock. I never cared if the merger went through or not, I was just doing my job."

"Maybe the killer doesn't plan to leave any potential witnesses."

He did the eye trick again. "Nah," he said. "I can't see it. Why go through all the trouble to be mysterious? Besides, I'm not so sure there's a murderer at all."

"Well, I'm sure Dost is dead."

"But how? All I'm saying is that if you can't explain how something happened, you certainly can't say anybody *did* it. I mean, just as many weird things happen by accident, instead of on purpose. What if Dost decided to jump off the roof or something?"

"That would be on purpose."

"You know what I mean. This is a big place. Jump out at the right angle, and you could get quite a distance away from the building."

"Not that far. And the snow on the roof is unbroken, too. I checked while I was outside."

"You should ask Barry about it," Bats said. "Tricks with the building, I mean. He knows everything about this place. Typical of him to run away when the shit gets thick."

"Barry?" I said. "Typical? You talk as if you know him."

"We were at college together. Business nerds at Princeton. There are science nerds and business nerds. I thought you knew."

"Why would I know?"

"Special Projects is supposed to know everything."

I looked at him. "Have you been talking to Carol Coretti?"

Bats grinned at me. "No, but I'd sure like to. Or are you asking me to stay out? I'm flattered you'd even be worried about a nearsighted, balding, skinny business nerd at all, Matt."

I could have told him not to waste his time, but it made better sense to get back to the point.

"Why do you say it's typical of Barry Dost to run away?"

"Because he's a stressed-out wreck, and has been since college. He worried about everything. I swear to God, one time a bunch of us went out to Chicago for a convention, and starting in Erie, Pennsylvania, Barry started worrying about whether there'd be a parking space available near the dorm."

"You were close, then."

"Not that close. There were five or six of us. We didn't want to blow up the administration building, we didn't do any drugs, unless you want to call beer a drug. We liked Neil Diamond better than Jefferson Airplane. So we found ourselves kind of falling together. We haven't kept in touch at all since we graduated."

"You didn't act as if you recognized each other last night."

"Barry might not have. That's another thing. He's always been incredibly self-absorbed. At the time, I thought it was just his father's getting married again that made him so jumpy—would she try to keep him away from the old man, the way his first stepmother did; would she sign the prenuptial agreement; our whole freshman year, he was in a tizzy over stuff like that—but even after the marriage it never went away."

"Did he ever express any hostility about his father?"

"Never. He *worshipped* his father. I've been thinking today that it's a good thing Barry wasn't going to college now."

"Why?"

Bats tented his fingers and leaned back. "Because Dost didn't get famous until later. I mean, we all knew he was loaded. The freaks would tell Barry, 'Your father's a rich pig, man,' and Barry could more or less shrug that off— the freaks ran that at anybody whose father wasn't a goddam sharecropper.

"But now it would be, 'Your father's G. B. Dost, the corporate raider, the financial pirate, the parasite of the American economy,' and all that happy horseshit. Barry'd probably get into screaming matches five times a day."

I felt the lump on the side of my head. "Don't sell him short," I said. "What did he think of Aranda?" I asked.

"He hated her guts. There was a bit of negotiation during the prenuptial-agreement deal—Barry gave me a play-by-play at the time, but I've forgotten it—and he was convinced she was, and I quote, 'a money-grubbing cunt.' Of course things might have changed. Also his hostility last night seemed directed at you."

"I seem to be bringing that out in people, lately."

Bats grinned. "You're still aces with me, Matt."

"Thanks, Bats. You're a real chum."

"That's me. Seriously, though, I think his problem is with anybody who was going to get between him and his father. I think Barry's problem always was that he didn't think he was good enough to be the son of G. B. Dost. And I don't think that kind of thing happens without the father at least unconsciously confirming it, how about you?"

"I don't know," I said. "My father was the white Bill Cosby."

"That's why you turned out perfect, I suppose."

"Precisely. But Barry's father is now dead. Messily and mysteriously. He's beyond impressing or living up to. Where does that leave Barry?"

Bats shifted uncomfortably in his chair. "Okay. I said a little while ago that Barry hadn't changed at all since college. I can't *know* that, okay? I've heard his running PR for his father has really done a lot for him—at least that was the word when your people checked out the Dost People (there they are again) before we scheduled this meeting. So I don't know for sure."

"Go by what you do know. The Barry Dost you knew in college, and what you saw last night."

Bats took a deep breath. "All right. If something like this happened to the Barry Dost I knew, it's my admittedly amateur opinion that it would send him right off the deep end. He might do anything."

"Like conk somebody on the head and run off into hiding?"

Bats nodded. "Exactly like that," he said. "I wouldn't be surprised if it all ended up in a mental hospital somewhere."

"The way things are going, I'll have the next cell."

"Hey, not you. Perfect people do not go nuts."

I handed it over to Ralph, who got Bats's declarations

that he had seen and heard nothing for the record, then we let Bats go.

When the door closed behind him, Ralph turned to me. "Boy, you guys have an *act*."

"What do you mean?"

"Abbot and Costello. Rowan and Martin."

"Martin and Van Buren. See, I can do it with you, too."

"I don't want to do it. I'm in way over my head, and all of a sudden my lifeguard starts a comedy act with one of the suspects."

"That wasn't comedy, that was repartee. New York City banter."

"It doesn't matter what you call it," Ralph insisted.

"You are so right. What matters is that it works. New Yorkers of my generation have been absolutely corrupted by David Letterman."

"What are you talking about?"

"I'm talking about the attitude that prevails in the Big City today, as personified by that gap-toothed jerk."

"You wouldn't say that if he was on *your* Network."

"See, you're doing it, too. What's important is to be *hip*. And the only way to be *hip* is to scorn everything. Because if you take anything seriously, if you *care* about anything, if you think anything is *worthwhile*, if you *believe* in anything, if you *love* anything, somebody might come along and laugh at you. And of course being a laugher is so much *hipper* than being a laughee."

"So you laugh at a murder," Ralph said.

"If you want somebody like Bats to talk to you about it, you do. You saw how he squirmed when you called him on it, and he had to admit, yes, he might have some un*hip* human decency left in him?"

"I thought this guy was your friend."

"He is."

"Why? If he's like that?"

"My point is, we're *all* like that. Then half of us go to group therapy just so we can be serious about something."

"Do you, ah . . .?"

I laughed. "No, I don't. I pick out helpless deputy sheriffs and unload my troubles on them. It's a lot cheaper than therapy. Who's next on the hit parade?"

He checked his list. "Wilberforce."

"Oh, goody," I said. "I've been meaning to ask him something."

Then the door opened and there he was. He was dressed for court, brown double-breasted suit, tie, brown shoes, wire-framed glasses polished to a steely glint, the whole number. It was intended either as a compliment to us or as a warning, I wasn't sure which.

Wilberforce strode to his chair and sat. He didn't wait for any questions.

"Cobb, I must take exception to the way you are handling this whole thing."

"I'm not handling anything," I told him. "I'm simply assisting Deputy Ingersoll."

"Nonsense." He turned that dead, gray-pink face on Ralph. "I'm sorry, young man, but we won't get anywhere until we all acknowledge that it's nonsense."

"Oh, I think we're getting somewhere," Ralph told him. "I'm getting good at Network vice-presidents."

Wilberforce gave up on him and turned back to me. "That is part of what I'm talking to you about. What could possibly have possessed you, attacking Haskell Freed that way?"

"I told him what possessed me. Why? Did you try to pull an insider-trading scam with Network stock, too?"

Charles Wilberforce is probably the most self-possessed man I've ever known. I've only seen him lose control once, and that was the time. "Don't be ridic— How dare you— Haskell tried to—"

"He tried to, and he admitted trying to. What did he tell you?"

Wilberforce opened his mouth.

"Never mind, I don't care. Just don't go jumping to any conclusions before you get the whole story."

Wilberforce closed his eyes, puffed out his cheeks, nodded and let the air go. When he was done, there was no sign he'd ever been upset. "Yes," he said. "Perhaps that will be best. Give me the whole story."

"No. You are a *suspect*, Charlie. A suspect. We ask questions, you answer."

His eyes narrowed. "You are going about this in the wrong way, Cobb."

"Good," I said. "Now we're back where we started. Tell me everything you did and saw and heard last night."

"Eventually, they'll get us out of here; when we get back to the Network, you'll still have to work with Freed and me."

"Unless I decide to tell the Feds, and Haskell goes to jail. What is it with you people? Are you all in this together, or what? I for one am a lot more concerned about living to be gotten out of here than about what's going to happen at the Network when I do."

Wilberforce said, "Hmpf," and crossed his arms over his chest.

"Now tell us about last night."

He did, in detail. His memory of our little excursion to the front stairs matched mine in every detail, which was gratifying but no help.

"Is that all?" he asked.

Ralph said, "Yes." I said, "Not quite."

The look in Wilberforce's eyes led me to think that maybe I ought to think twice about going back to the Network when this was over, at that. Maybe I could get a job as a deputy sheriff.

"Why in the name of God did you insist on seeing Dost's body?" I asked.

"Quite simple. I wanted to confirm for myself that it was indeed the body of G. B. Dost."

"By that time, Deputy Ingersoll had identified the body, *I* had identified the body, his wife, his partner and lifelong friend, *and* his servants all had identified the body as the remains of G. B. Dost."

"You might be mistaken. The others might be lying for some nefarious purpose. Now that I think of it, there's no reason why *you* shouldn't have been lying too. I don't see why I should trust you any more than you seem to trust me. Perhaps Dost was still alive, and a dead double substituted for him. How should I know? I just felt it my duty to my employer . . ." He didn't actually say *a duty some of us obviously feel more strongly than others,* he just paused long enough so my conscience, if I had one, could fill it in for me. ". . . my duty to make sure. That is all."

"So you looked." Wilberforce nodded. "And?"

"It was Dost."

"Thanks. That's what I thought."

Wilberforce got up and left. It was a struggle, but I managed to cork my laughter until the door closed behind him.

"What's so funny now?" Ralph asked.

"Nothing. After that lecture I just gave you, I should be ashamed of myself for laughing. I am ashamed of myself. It's just that I never dreamed Wilberforce would come up with something so *romantic.* Nefarious substitution plots, for God's sake. There's an imagination somewhere behind that dead face."

Ralph scratched his head. "Since you let that Freed guy off the hook, I don't see where we have anything better."

"You're a killjoy, you know that, Ralph?"

"Just trying to keep my mind on my job. I've got it tougher than you have, you know. You're trying to decide which one of them did it. I've got to watch you and decide whether *you* did it."

"Hmm," I said. "Is this the same guy who was begging me to help him, this morning?"

"I still need your help. I've been helped already. I completely agree with you about the trickiness of what's going on here. It's just that watching you work, I'm beginning to think you're the trickiest guy I ever laid eyes on."

"It's the only way I know to do this sort of thing."

"Oh, I understand. And I don't really think you did it. I just want to be absolutely fair, and let you know you're still on the list."

"I'd be disappointed in you if I weren't," I told him.

Carol Coretti was next. She had no axes to grind, no lecture to deliver. She just sat prettily with her hands in her lap and answered questions. After the meeting with me and Wilberforce, she had gone to bed, alone, and slept until the hubbub over finding Dost's body awakened her. She had nothing helpful to offer, no observations or opinions.

"Have you had anything further to do with Mrs. Dost?"

"No. I haven't been exactly avoiding her, but I haven't been lingering around her, either. Should I?"

I begged her pardon.

"Do you want me to spy on her or something? I mean, I wouldn't *sleep* with her or anything, but I certainly know how to *flirt*."

"I know," I said. "You were flirting with me in the car."

She looked at me sadly. "I wasn't, you know. But it's not your fault. Men are sex-crazy by nature. If a woman isn't actually hostile to you, you think we're flirting. It's a choice all gay women have to make, you know. And since I don't *hate* men, I decided to put up with occasional charges of false advertising. I'm sorry."

"Don't mention it," I said. "Live and learn. Why are you willing to flirt with Mrs. Dost?"

"Well, only if it will *help*. If you think I could learn something that would help you figure this out. I don't like being stuck with a murderer any more than you do."

"Oh. Thanks for the sentiment, but don't do anything just yet. We want to talk to Mrs. Dost first."

"Oh. Okay, Matt," she said. She smiled shyly and wiggled her fingers in good-bye. It sure looked like flirting to me.

I turned to Ralph. "All right, you sex-crazy bastard, who's next?"

"You want to talk to Roxanne Schick?"

"Nah. We talked to her all morning."

"Okay. I can't see a motive for her, anyway. She's got as much money as Dost had, for God's sake."

"Not quite. Close, though."

"Well, that leaves Jack Bromhead and the widow."

"Oh, let's save the widow for last."

Jack Bromhead limped in and sat in the chair. About every three seconds he winced. Ralph asked him if he was all right.

"Oh, yeah," Bromhead grunted. "It's just about time to take the next dose of medicine, you know. I'll take it as soon as we're done here. Codeine makes me a little dopey, I'd rather be alert to answer your questions."

"I'd like to take a look at your ankle," I said.

"What?"

"I'd like to see your ankle. That it's really sprained. If it is, it's probably less likely you killed him. I mean, as far as we can tell, the body got out there by magic, but a sprained ankle makes everything harder, probably magic, too. On the other hand, if it's a nice, pink, healthy ankle, we can call it established you're a dirty rotten liar, and go on from there."

Bromhead laughed. "This is your day for pissing people off, ain't it, boy?"

"I figure I've used up about six months' worth, so far. Come on, Jack, you must have known this would be checked. If not by us, then by the regular investigators."

"What if I tell you it never crossed my mind for a second that I would be suspected of killing my oldest and closest friend?"

"Then I'd say if you meant that, there's no way you were smart enough to be G. B. Dost's right-hand man."

Bromhead laughed. "All right, all right. I can see why Gabby wanted to hire you. Go ahead, but *you* take it off. Hurts like hell when I bend over."

I knelt and unlaced the boot. He'd had it tight enough to keep a broken bone in place. I knew he wasn't faking as soon as I pulled the boot off. I was as gentle as I could be, but Bromhead gasped and turned white. No one could fake that.

"I'm sorry," I said.

"Hell with that. You started, now finish."

I eased down the sock to reveal an ankle swollen to twice its size. It was an old sprain, and a bad one, the bruises black where they weren't turning green.

"Jesus," I said, looking at it. "I don't know how you manage to walk."

"They grow us tough out west. I think, though, boys, you're going to have to help me get back upstairs. That boot's not going back on today."

"You should have gone to the hospital when this happened," Ralph said. "You still should."

"Doctors. It's getting better without them. Soak it in cold water, take the medicine, lace the boot up tight. I'll be fine. Besides, I won't be going to any hospitals or anywhere else until they dig us out of here. Heard that Freed guy say something about snowmobiles. Huh. Snowmobiles are more like boats than anything else. You sure can't get one up a hill this high."

Bromhead insisted he was up to being questioned, so we

asked away. The first thing I wanted to hear about was Barry Dost. Bromhead's assessment tallied pretty well with Bats Blefary's.

"But he's been doing real good, lately, Barry has. Lots of ideas. Must be those books he reads, future stuff. But he got his father using a lot of new PR stuff, to keep the animals happy, you know? It was like pulling teeth to get Gabby to do some of that stuff, but Barry stood up to his old man, and Barry proved himself right."

"Did Mrs. Dost ever sign the prenuptial agreement?"

"How'd you know about that?"

"An inspired guess," I said.

"All right, all right. I never told anyone how I sniffed out an oil well, either. Yeah, she signed it. That's why I really don't think Aranda had anything to do with this."

"What do you mean?"

"Don't you guys have a thing called *cui bono*? Means 'who's better off?'"

"That's what it means."

"Yeah, well, this *cui* don't *bono* enough."

Ralph said, "Doesn't she get *anything*?"

"She gets the house in Palm Springs and the apartment in New York. She gets five million bucks, and another five million insurance. Ten million with double indemnity."

"You're talking about twenty million worth of stuff, after taxes. That sounds like a pretty significant *bono* to me. A kid I grew up with was knifed to death over a ten-dollar basketball."

"You don't know Aranda. She likes to buy things. Horses, like that. She throws parties at the Four Seasons. Have you ever seen a bunch of astrologers *eat*?" He shook his head. "They may be spiritual as all hell, but they don't forget the flesh."

"Still and all," Ralph said. He was appalled at the idea of twenty million bucks not being enough. I would have been, too, but I had been inured by long exposure to Show Business.

Bromhead said, "Three years. Four and half, maybe five, if she sells the real estate. No, I'll tell you, darlin' Aranda had a lot more *bono* going for her when Gabby was alive."

"So who gets the rest?"

"Barry. I get a little, but mostly it goes to Barry."

"If twenty million isn't enough, how much is a little to you?"

"Not to me, to Aranda. I honestly don't know how much Gabby left me, and I don't much care. Following him, I've made *plenty* of money. But I'd give it all to have him back." He looked at me with moist eyes. "And if you don't believe that, Mister, you can go straight to hell. Both of you."

"Why did he have a surf-casting rod?"

"Huh?"

"In the tackle room. There's a big old surf-casting rod. Be a hell of a toss to get that into the nearest surf."

"Oh," Bromhead said. "You ought to slow down a little around corners, boy. It's easy. See, more and more, Gabby was using this place as a home base. Guess he liked it. Barry picked it out for him, you know, back when he was in college. Anyway. Gabby never really knew where he was going to go next, but if it was near the ocean, he'd want to bring that rod with him. It was his favorite one."

"The line on it's all tangled," I said.

Bromhead frowned. "That wasn't like Gabby. He always took care of his equipment."

"Well," I sighed. "Just another little mystery for us."

I gave Bromhead my shoulder as we walked to the door, then recruited Calvin Gowe and Bats Blefary to help him up to his room where he could take his painkiller and soak his foot.

I went to the bar and made a bourbon and soda for myself. Ralph had one too. He looked as exhausted as I felt. I had no idea how guys like Hercule Poirot and Doctor Fell managed it. Yes, I did. By not being real, that's how they managed it.

"Drinking on duty," Ralph said, looking appreciatively at his glass. "Bad."

"Just one didn't hurt. I needed it."

"Time for the widow?"

"Time for the widow."

13

Now here she is, the woman you've all been waiting for. . . .
—Pat Sajak, "Wheel of Fortune" (syndicated)

Aranda Dost had been able to throw together something quiet and suitable for mourning. She wore a black turtleneck, gray skirt, black stockings, black wedgies. She looked like the kind of English teacher junior high school kids get flaming crushes on. She sat down, shook her hair back, sniffed imperiously, looked at us and said, "Well?"

I had ruffled a lot of feathers today. Part of it was inevitable—murder is a very un-nice activity, and you can't be sweet about chasing someone who's committed one. On the other hand, you can handle your face and voice and diction to keep the necessary offensiveness to a minimum, and I deliberately hadn't done that.

It was all part of a brain game I was playing with Aranda Dost. I didn't know who'd killed her husband, but I had a strong feeling that she knew things I wanted to know that she'd just as soon not tell.

She figured to be tough. Not physically, but mentally and emotionally. People who are less-than-tough don't last as long in show business as Aranda had. And women who

121

are less than tough rarely survive the sharklike frenzy that surrounds a newly eligible millionaire.

So I wanted her thinking about how tough *I* was. I wanted as many people as possible to walk out of here saying Cobb was chewing steel wool and spitting out nails. I wanted her braced for an all-out attack.

Which would not come.

"Mrs. Dost," I said, "I want to apologize for disrupting your household like this. And for anything I've said or done today to make you upset." I spread my hands. "I was upset, myself. I respected your husband for a long time, and although I only spent a few hours in his company, I found myself coming to like him quite a bit."

"Yes," she said. She showed me a brave little smile. "Gabriel was the most charming man I ever knew. I accept your apology, Mr. Cobb. But I thought we had agreed to be Matt and Aranda. And, of course, Ralph." She dazzled him with her teeth.

I smiled back. "Aranda, then. I won't try to kid you—the situation is pretty grim. We've learned some useful things today, but it hasn't been easy, and it hasn't been enough. Unless you have some information for us, I'm afraid we're all going to have to go to bed tonight with the killer still loose."

"I don't know what information *I* could possibly give you."

"Neither do we. We just have to get as much as we can and sift it out later. Why don't we start with, oh, I don't know—tell us about what you did yesterday."

"All day?"

"Sure. Take my word for it, sometimes this is a lot easier if you begin at the beginning."

"Oh, I know all about your experience, Matt. Gabriel didn't like to go into negotiations without knowing as much as possible about the people he'd be dealing with."

"Then you probably know I have even more experience

answering these kinds of questions than I do asking them. So take my word for it, and begin at the beginning."

So she did. I learned a lot of helpful hints about throwing a house party, especially if it involves supervising servants, but not much about the case. She took us right through the party to her bedtime, leaving a trail of sweetness and light behind her. If she noticed Barry's snit with me, she didn't mention it. She didn't mention Carol Coretti at all.

The questions went on. As far as she knew, Dost was under no unusual pressure ("Of course, the *usual* pressure around here would crush a normal man *flat*," she said); none of his business enemies had shown any sign of mental instability, there had been no threats out of the ordinary.

"Except, of course, for that letter to the Network." Aranda frowned. "That was a little frightening, even though it didn't make any threats. At least not directly. And it wasn't sent to him."

I raised an eyebrow. "But he was frightened by it?"

"Oh, not him, me. *I* was frightened by it. I'm frightened by people who choose to live twisted lives when it's so easy to open up to the goodness of the Cosmos. But Gabriel was such a solid man, such a *whole* man, that things like that just didn't register with him. He wasn't frightened of anything, in all the time I knew him. Jack Bromhead is the same way."

"Did your husband always talk about his business with you?"

"Whenever I asked. I didn't ask often. There was so *much* of it, you know." She waved that away. "I kept up pretty well with the Network negotiations, though. I was interested because it's show business. I sang on the Network a couple of times."

Ralph snapped himself up straight in his chair. "That

was *you?*" he said. "On 'The Theodore Farnsworth Show?' Singing a song about a waterfall? I never dreamed."

Aranda smiled at him. "Have I changed all that much, Ralph?"

"No, it's not that. I've always thought you looked famil-iar, and don't forget, I was just a little kid at the time—"

"Oops," I said. Aranda shushed me and told Ralph to go on.

"Well, I wasn't *that* little a kid. Maybe ten years old."

"You're not helping yourself, Ralph," I told him.

"Anyway, if I'd had chart records and sung on TV, I'd tell people about it. Everybody. That's something to be proud of."

"Thank you," she said. "You're sweet to say such kind things to an old lady."

Ralph blushed. "I'm sorry about that."

"Don't be. I was just teasing you. You *are* sweet. I can see why your uncle is so proud of you. But I'm afraid that in the circles I've moved in since I met Gabriel, where people make deals worth a billion dollars during one phone call, and affect the lives of millions of people, maybe whole countries, having a hit record or two in your past seems kind of quaint. I'd gotten out of the habit of telling people about it. It's so much nicer when someone like you or Matt remembers."

"I know it's very early to ask this, but have you given any thought to the future now?" If this had been the nasty Matt Cobb she'd been expecting, the question would have been, "What are going to do now that your husband's dead?" Which she wouldn't have answered.

Now, she answered readily. "It is early," she said, "but I suppose I might as well begin thinking about it. I won't be running Gabriel's empire, or deciding who will, and I'm very glad of that. That all goes to Barry, poor boy, I hope he's up to it. I signed a pre-nuptial agreement that will

124

leave me well provided for—it's more than any normal person could ever need."

Ralph shot me a look. I hoped Aranda hadn't seen it.

She went on. "Maybe I'll go back to singing. I still vocalize every morning, you know. It's one thing not to use a talent, but it's another to let it rust away. Don't you think so?"

"I couldn't say," I told her. "I don't have any talent."

"Don't play coy, Matt. I suspect you're bursting with all kinds of talents." Her mock scolding look and the shaking of her golden head made me wish Carol Coretti were here to tell me if this was flirting or not.

"Of course, if I *do* sing again, I'm going to do it under another name."

"Why's that?" Ralph wanted to know.

"Because I am a good singer, you know. I have a certain amount of pride—I'd call it artistic pride, if that didn't sound so pretentious—and I'd want people to relate to me as a *singer,* rather than as a billionaire's wife. Widow."

After the word "widow," she let out a little gasp, as if appalled by the sound of it, and by what it meant. She stared into space for a few seconds, then turned back to me.

"I'm sorry, Matt," she said. "Is there anything else I can help with?"

"Maybe," I said. "We'd really like to talk to Barry, and, let's face it, he may be in danger, running around the house on his own like that. If there's any way you could influence him to rejoin the group, we'd appreciate it."

Aranda shook her head.

"You won't do it?" Ralph said.

"It's not that. It's that I don't really have any influence with Barry."

"Don't you get along?"

"Oh, we get along all right. At least, for the last few years we have. There was a time Barry really disliked me. I don't think he ever got over his father and mother splitting up. Most children in that situation hang on to mad dreams that their parents will get back together, but Barry clung to them long into adulthood."

"Why hold it against you?" I asked. "You didn't break his parents up."

"No, but I got in the way after Gabriel's second marriage ended and he was free to go back to Barry's mother. I'm speaking from Barry's point of view, you understand."

"How about your point of view?"

"My point of view was that I'd gotten hold of the finest man in the world, and nothing was going to—going to come between us."

Aranda started to mist up, but controlled herself. "I'm sorry," she said. "After that outburst this morning, I made a vow that I *would* control myself."

"It's perfectly natural," I said.

"It's perfectly foolish," she snapped. "Haven't I studied? Haven't I experienced? If a friend of mine had lost someone, I would be at her side telling her that death is only a transition; that the essence, the soul, if you like, of the person she'd loved was on a different plane, a beautiful place out in space, waiting to enter the world again small and innocent as a little baby."

When I was in high school, I used to belong to a science-fiction film club. We met Saturday evenings in a freezing cold cellar below a restaurant in the East Thirties. One day, the guy who ran the place showed up all excited because he'd gotten hold of a very early talkie, *F.P.1 Does Not Answer,* also known as *F.P.1 Antwortet Nicht.* It was a German picture, shot simultaneously in German, French, and English. It started out fine, but about a half hour into the film, the faces of most of the actors changed, and they all began speaking German. It was a very unsettling experience, and the reason I am reasonably fluent in four languages today. I wanted to minimize the chances of that sort of bewilderment befalling me again.

But by golly, here it was. The switch this time wasn't from English to German, but from sense to gibberish. I was not, however, going to run out and become fluent in New Age. Not in this life, anyway.

She went on at great length, going so far as to lament that with Gabriel dead, the chances of Derek getting his own show on the Network were now greatly reduced. Derek was her trance channeler. He had a hot line to Imhotep. She offered to lend Ralph and me some of her crystals, to "help us get in touch with ourselves."

Ralph said, "No, thanks, ma'am. My mother told me if I spent too much time getting in touch with myself, I'd go blind."

So much for the respectful approach. Aranda drew up as if she'd been slapped. I, of course, was unable to keep myself from dissolving in hysterics, thereby blowing my chance to slap Ralph down and switch this to a game of good-cop, bad-cop.

"I see," she said angrily. "Throughout history, small minds have always stood in the way of their own enlightenment."

I tried to apologize and start some kind of damage control, but Aranda wouldn't have it. The fact that I couldn't stop laughing didn't help.

She pointed a red-tipped finger at me. "Last night, Mr. Cobb, you challenged me to make a prediction for you. Here it is: Gabriel will speak to you. Before you leave this house, my husband will send a message that will help you solve his murder."

"Any notion as to when this might be?" I asked.

"He'd hate to sleep through it," Ralph said.

Aranda said quietly, "I had thought better of you, Ralph. The message will reach you, Mr. Cobb."

"I can hardly wait," I assured her. It was too late to

apologize, anyway. "I wish you'd predict that Barry would get a message to come in from the cold."

"It seems rather humiliating to ask this in my own house," she said, "but may I go now?"

I decided to let it slide that it was Barry's house now, or would be as soon as the will was read. "In a minute," I said. "One more question."

"What more could there be?"

"Did you make a pass at Carol Coretti last night?"

"A pass? What kind of pass?"

"A two-handed bounce pass," I said. "A *sexual* pass, for crying out loud. Did you?"

"I've had quite enough insults from you, Mr. Cobb."

"It's a shame, I've got plenty left. Did you come on to her?"

"Absolutely not. Am I accused of being a lesbian, now?"

"Actually, no. Miss Coretti is, but she doesn't think you are. That's why she thought it so strange you'd proposition her."

"I never did. And you're a fool to listen to that kind of accusation. Those people are desperate and pathetic, and likely to say anything. If I'd known, I wouldn't have had her in my house."

Her house, again.

"If you like, I can have Miss Coretti brought here. She might apologize." Or she might call you a lying bitch, I thought.

"No, thank you. I prefer to ignore the whole matter. Will that be all?"

"For now," I said.

"They can't plow us out of here soon enough! *God*, I wish they were here now."

She stormed out. I watched her go, thinking it was nice to end the day on something we all could agree on.

14

Two's company, indisputably. Two's company, irrefutably.
Elaine Stritch and Donald Sinden, "Two's Company"
(London Weekend Television and A&E)

The entire gathering ate dinner in a wordless snit. Even
Bats Blefary, who wasn't especially mad at anybody, gave
up conversation as a bad idea after a few sallies.

"How's the food holding out?" he asked Aunt Agnes
brightly. Not the most tactful question, you'll notice, but
maybe he'd caught it from me.

"Plenty of everything except fresh vegetables," she said.
"We did plan to have you people up here for ten days, if
necessary."

"Good," Bats said. "That's good."

I wasn't mad at anybody, either, just distracted. I think it
was safe to say, though, that I was the least popular person
in the room. Roxanne, Carol, and Bats might have been
willing to lift a finger to save my life, and Ralph, of course.
But judging from the looks I got from the others, I would
have been a fool to eat any of the roast beef or mashed
potatoes or gravy or string beans if I hadn't seen them
served from a common dish.

I was glad when it was late enough to go to bed. Keeping in mind my injunction about traveling in groups of three or more, I went up with the Normans, which made for a jolly trip. Before I went, I told the gang to remember what I'd said about fortifying their doors.

I took my own advice, propping a conveniently sized antique chair under the doorknob and backing that up with a Samoyed who knows how to watch a door. Then I took a shower, dried off, and lay down on the bed.

So. What have I accomplished today? Besides making everybody mad at me, I thought. Well, we taught Haskell Freed a little humility. Proved Jack Bromhead really had sprained his ankle.

Or had we?

I thought it over. I'd taken a picture of every other damned thing today, I wished I'd taken a picture of Jack Bromhead's ankle. Could he have done the nasty business to Gabby Dost and *then* hurt his ankle? I didn't think so. That greenish tinge Bromhead showed around the edges of his bruise only set in after a few days, in my experience. But then, what the hell did I know? I wasn't a doctor. Suppose Bromhead had some kind of condition that made the green show up early.

Forget it, Cobb, I told myself. Forget it. You can only wait until the people with the right resources get here. *They'll* worry about the answers to questions like that, and *you'll* be in jail for impersonating an officer and tampering with evidence and God knows what all, so you'll have other problems on your mind.

Thinking of Bromhead's bruises led me to remember the bruises on Dost's back. Dammit, I'd forgotten to ask the widow if she knew how they'd gotten there; if flailing yourself on the back with a stick like some medieval monk was part of Dost's idea of a good time.

I didn't really think that was the explanation—the marks were too few and too symmetrical—but it was the only thing I could think of when I saw them, and I should have at least *asked*. I should have asked Jack Bromhead, too.

Wonderful, I thought, now I have an agenda for tomorrow. Maybe Dost would flash me the answer from a Higher Plane.

Meanwhile, I reflected on today's *really big* achievement—catching Aranda Dost in a whacking great lie. The question presented itself: What, if anything, did this lie mean? And, assuming it *does* mean something, what do I do about it?

By the door, Spot rose to a crouch and growled low in his throat. A half-second later, there was a knock on the door. I rolled out of bed and stuffed myself into the red gym shorts I'd been such a hit in this morning. I had visions of angry villagers out there with torches, but if they didn't like my attire, they could lump it. Whoever it was could lump it.

I walked to the door and grabbed the chair with both hands, both to get it out of Spot's way, if necessary, and to pick up as a weapon, if Spot turned out not to be enough.

The knocking was louder, this time.

"Who is it?" I demanded.

"It's me, Cobb, Roxanne. Open up."

"Who's with you?"

"Nobody."

"Is that the way you listen, you little twerp?"

"Yeah. Well, I didn't expect the Spanish Inquisition to keep me out here in the hallway."

My line was "*Nobody* expects the Spanish Inquisition," but I didn't feel like going into it. Instead, I said, "I'm not dressed."

"I've seen you naked, Cobb. Come on, let me in."

I called off Spot and moved the chair away from the floor. Roxanne bounced in wearing a bright-yellow pair of fuzzy Dr. Denton's, complete with feet. She looked like a five-foot, three-inch teddy bear. She sat in the armchair and said, "Hi!"

"Hi, yourself. To what do I owe the honor?"

"I was lonely. I wanted to see Spot." She was ruffling the fur of his neck, something he loves more than steak.

"Would you like to borrow him for the night? You're old friends, after all."

She thought it over for a second. "Well, as long as I'm here, I might as well talk to you. You look like you could use a friendly face."

"*As if* I could use a friendly face."

Roxanne nodded. "That's a good way to get one, too, correcting people's grammar." She leaned forward. "Seriously, though, Cobb, I've never seen you so weird. And that's saying something."

"I don't like sharing a roof with a murderer."

"You've been at close quarters with murderers before."

"Claustrophobia, then. I don't like the idea of being in a place I can't leave. I think we're all starting to get a little nuts on that score."

"I sure am. But it's more than that, with you. Could it be you were bracing yourself to take a run at Carol Coretti, and now you're left with a set of frustrated hormones?"

"I've gone years with frustrated hormones," I said. "There's nothing wrong with me."

"Too late. You should have said that three minutes ago, if you wanted it to be believable. Not that I would have believed it then, either. I *know* you too well, Cobb."

"All right. Maybe I was going to suggest to Carol we get together when we got back to the city. Maybe I did get saved by an eyelash from having my nose pushed in, however gently. That should make me glad, right? I don't even know why I'm discussing this."

"Something about me," Roxanne intoned, "compels honesty from those weaker of intellect. Anyway, it doesn't matter. I was just trying to poison your mind against her this morning. I was just going by instinct. It was, you know, badinage. The only way we seem to talk anymore."

"I have the same problem with Bats Blefary."

"I'll let him worry about that. I'm more worried about you."

"I'm fine," I said again, but I didn't mean it.

"You don't mean that," said the little psychic. "I know what your problem is."

"Oh, tell me, Doctor, please."

"Not so fast. Do you think I've been spending all this money on colleges just to *tell* people things? Not at all. If we don't use the Socratic method, it won't work."

I figured, what the hell. I'm a product of my time, a child of the Me Generation. Why shouldn't we talk about Me for a while? Especially if worrying about Me would take my mind off the image of Gabby Dost bleeding into the virgin snow.

"May I relax while we talk?"

Roxanne was gracious. "By all means," she said. I lay down on the bed and laced my fingers behind my head.

"All right, then," she said. "How old was I when you met me?"

"Not quite sixteen."

"What condition was I in?"

"You were a wreck. Strung out on heroin. Dirty, scared, and sick."

"Who got me to the hospital? Who helped me kick? Who ran the pimp out of town when he tried to take me back? Who let me have two more good years with my father?"

"I did. I was doing my job."

"Your job was to find me. None of the rest of that stuff. Now, your girlfriend at the time was Monica Teobaldi, famous actress, correct?"

"She wasn't so famous then, and it was more complicated than that, but that's basically true."

"And what happened to Monica?"

"She got a part she'd been up for, and took off for L.A."

"She left a *message* on your *machine*. She dumped you like a hot brick without even saying *good-bye*."

"Right."

"How old was I at the time?"

"Nineteen."

"What happened between us the night Monica left?"

I sat up. "Look, Rox, this isn't much fun—"

"Shut up," she ordered. "It isn't supposed to be fun. What happened?"

"You came to my apartment."

"Yeah. I came to your apartment. What did we do, play Parcheesi all night?"

"You know what we did. Rox, come on . . . "

She was implacable. "Say it."

I said it. "We made love."

"We made what?"

"Love."

"Thank you." She batted her eyelashes. "Was it good for you, Darling?"

"Don't you remember?"

"I remember fine how it was for me. We're talking about you. On a scale of one to ten."

"Twelve," I said.

"Don't joke, Cobb."

"It was terrific. You were there. You turned me into a gibbering idiot. What more do you need?"

"We're making excellent progress."

"Oh, goody."

"Now let's talk about the women you've been involved with since then."

"Dammit, Rox, I am not going to rate every woman I've ever slept with on a scale of one to ten just to satisfy your curiosity."

"I don't want you to. I just want to know what happened to the relationships. Llona Hall?"

"Are you serious?"

"I have never been more serious in my life."

"She connived at murder. Unprovable. She left the country with some incredible amount of money and bought an island somewhere. I don't know where."

"Okay. Morally lacking. You dumped her. Now that lawyer upstate. Well, downstate from here, but you know what I mean."

"Eve Bowen. She's the D.A. there now. She's going to run for Congress. She said she couldn't be having an affair with a campaign going on."

"So why didn't you get married?"

"She didn't think the voters would understand the kind of work I do."

"So she dumped you, because you dripped sleaze on her ambitions."

"How poetic."

"Thank you. How about Wendy Ichimi, who, incidentally, is exactly one month younger than I am?"

"She's always traveling the world with an ice show."

"Dumped you because of her career."

"Right."

"And finally, the librarian, Kenni Clayton."

"How the hell did you know about her?"

"A person named 'Schick' can always get answers at the Network. What happened to her?"

"She got weirded out," I said.

"Too kinky for her?"

"No, it was something I did."

"I'm waiting."

"I—set a friend of hers up to be killed. I didn't mean it that way. She was a murderer and a drug dealer, the friend was, and she'd admitted it to me, but there was no way to prove it for the law unless she cooperated. So I wanted to put pressure on her to make her confess. One of the people she killed was the nephew of a Mafia don, and I told him where she was."

"So he killed her."

"Not exactly. She mistook a cop I'd also told about her for a Mafia hit man, ran into the subway trying to get away, and fell off the platform in front of an uptown Number One train."

"And you felt guilty."

"No. I didn't feel one tiny little bit guilty. That's what weirded Kenni out. She was always looking at me funny."

"She's got a lot of nerve," Roxanne said, suddenly indignant.

"What happened to the Socratic method?"

"My *mother* killed somebody, and you pushed her over the edge from psycho to total mental vegetable, and I never looked at you funny."

"Yeah," I said. I'd never thought of Memory Lane as such a bumpy road. "Well, Kenni's life has been populated by nicer people than yours or mine."

"Still, what did she want you to do, let her get *away* with it?"

"No. She just couldn't understand why I had to be the one to stop her."

"What a wimp." Roxanne went on in this vein under her breath for a few minutes, while I considered the question. I had to be the one because I was the only one who could. If I hadn't done anything to stop Kenni's friend, then the harm she inflicted on anybody else (and this woman had an infinite capacity for harm) would be at least partially my fault. *That* would make me feel guilty. I know that there are millions of decent, honest people who feel differently, including, I suppose, every defense lawyer alive, but that's my point of view, and I like myself better for it.

"Anyway," Roxanne said, as though we'd never digressed at all, "here comes the sixty-four-thousand-dollar question: *Is it not true you could have made it work with any of those women if you'd really wanted to?"*

I was indignant. "No!" I said. "How could I possibly have made it work with Llona?"

"Okay, okay, forget her. What about the rest? All you had to do about Monica or Wendy Ichimi was quit the Network—you always say you hate this damn job, anyway—and go along and be their manager or something. Women in show business have supported their men for years. It's like a tradition."

"A better tradition is when everyone supports himself."

"Touché," she said.

"Oh, hell," I said. "I wasn't talking about you. Of course it's okay to take care of your *children*."

"That's swell. But children like me grow up, and we've still got the money. Then what happens?"

"They take over the family business. Or they take up Hare Krishna or radical politics. Or they become philanthropists, or patrons of the arts. Depends a lot on character."

"Okay, enough about me. Back to you. You could have made the politician happy by delivering a whole lot of leverage on Network personnel to her. Nothing like good media coverage to further a political career."

I sat up. "Do you really think I would do that?"

"Would she want you to?"

"No!" At least, I didn't think so.

Roxanne just made a skeptical little "mmmm" and went on. "The librarian would have been easiest of all. All you would have had to do was pretend a little remorse over what happened to her friend. White lies are a time-honored way for most people to keep a relationship on an even keel. But not for you. Not with her. Why not?"

"I thought you were going to tell me why I've been so grouchy."

"We're getting to that. Right now, I'm offering to tell you

why you keep failing to make these romances last. Do you want to know, or not?"

"Is there any way in the world, short of breaking your jaw, that I could keep you from telling me?"

She shook her head. "And even then, I would write it down."

"Then, please, do, tell me."

"It's me. You're in love with me, and that's what keeps you from doing anything final with anybody else."

I sat up and looked at her. "No problems in the ego department for you, are there?"

"Oodles. I just know the truth when I've spent a few years studying it. I'm the reason you're so uptight here, too. I told you we'd get around to it. You're afraid I'm in danger, and you're wondering how the fact that I'm not going to be able to sell the Network is going to affect me."

"Both those things could be true without my being in love with you."

"Ha! You've just got it in your head that I'm too young and too rich and you love me too much to take advantage of me, when maybe I don't really love you."

"You don't," I said.

Roxanne's voice was deadly. "Don't say that, Cobb. Never say that."

"That may be what it seems like to you, Rox, but it's not. I pulled you out of that hellhole you'd run away to, and I'm glad I did it. You were a kid, then, though, and you saw me as this white knight. Ever since, you've been telling me how great I am, how you owe me your life, you'd do anything for me. That's not love. Love is loving somebody in spite of his faults and weaknesses, not pretending they don't exist. Being perfect is too much pressure for a man to take."

"I know you have faults. For one thing, you're a complete asshole when it comes to women. For another thing, once you make up your mind about something, you never notice when things change."

"What do you mean?"

"I mean, I came to the same conclusion you did about three years ago. About praising you too much, making you uncomfortable. I stopped, but you never noticed. I've even tried being a sarcastic little bitch to get your attention, which did no good at all. Now I'm trying a direct approach. I don't know what's left, except maybe hitting you between the eyes with a two-by-four."

"What do you want from me, Rox?"

"Be honest with yourself. Am I right in what I've said here tonight, or not? And don't treat me like a kid. I'm long since a grown woman and I'm fighting for the man I love."

I looked at her again in the sleeper blanket. "I grant that you are a woman, and a hell of a one, if I may say so."

"Thank you," she said primly.

"But if that was the point you wanted to make, why did you come dressed like a one-year-old?"

"I didn't want to vamp you into anything."

"All men are sex-crazy," I said.

"Close enough."

I flopped back on the pillows and let out a breath. Be honest with myself, she said. I forced myself to be. And she was right. I'd been running from her for years now, for no damn good reason at all.

"It's scary, Rox," I said.

"Not as scary as the thought of blowing it all without giving it a try."

Not only was she rich and pretty, she was *smart*, too. I had the feeling there were going to be some interesting times ahead. I told her so.

"Great," she said. "Now move over and let me on the bed."

I took her in my arms and we kissed. After a few seconds, I started to laugh.

"What's so funny?" Roxanne wanted to know.

I grabbed a handful of yellow fuzz. "This," I said. "It's like making love to Winnie the Pooh."

She bit my nose. "Big detective. Can't even figure out how a zipper works."

I puzzled it out. I pulled the long zipper down slowly and carefully. After all, there was a treasure inside.

15

Come, let us reason together.
—Lyndon B. Johnson, televised speech

About 2:00 A.M. I said, "We'd better stop giggling and get some sleep."

Roxanne giggled. "We've got the rest of our lives to sleep," she said.

"And a long time after that, too."

She looked at me. Her eyes were big and bright in the dim lamplight. "You're morbid, Cobb," she said. "How could I love anybody as morbid as you are?"

"Beats me," I said. "Second thoughts already? You have your way with me—"

"Actually, I had a couple of ways with you."

"—and now you want to toss me aside, just because I'm morbid."

"Never," she said. "Be as morbid as you want. We can sleep in coffins for all I care."

"Do they make double coffins?"

"I'm rich, I'll get one custom-made."

"Swell. Any color velvet lining you like. Now let's get some sleep, okay?"

"Can't," she declared. "I'm hungry."

I yawned. "I think Spot's got some food left. Maybe he'll share."

"I'm serious, Cobb." She pushed me in the ribs.

"I'm serious, too. I didn't get a whole lot of sleep last night, and I had a busy day. And I'd better be just as busy tomorrow."

"What more could you *do*?"

I yawned again. "I'll think of something. Can't let the killer be busier than you are."

Roxanne winced. I hadn't meant to say that; hadn't meant to bring the killer in bed with us.

"Come down to the kitchen with me, Cobb. Dost gave us icebox-raiding privileges that first night, and I've never used mine."

"This is only the second night, Rox."

"I know, I know. Come on, I'll make you a cup of hot chocolate, you can relax. We'll bring Spot down, so we won't even be breaking your three-at-a-time rule."

"All right," I said. "God, two hours into the relationship, and I'm henpecked already."

"Get used to it," Roxanne said brightly. "It's good for you."

Roxanne climbed back into her teddy-bear suit, and I got into my sweats, and we took off for the kitchen.

The light switches in the hallway had little night-lights in them, enough to find our way to the kitchen by. The kitchen itself was pitch black—the round window in the swinging door might as well have been onyx. "Now," I said to Roxanne, "if I remember correctly, the light switch is to the right side of the door." I pushed inside and groped for the switch—this one wasn't lighted. As soon as I flicked it, a voice said, *"Freeze!"*

I blinked against the sudden light. Roxanne gave a little scream, Spot snarled. I blinked again, and found myself staring into the muzzles of a double-barreled shotgun, and the very angry, very frightened face of Barry Dost.

"Don't move, killer," Barry said.

"Anything you say."

"That's right, anything I say." Barry had rye bread, lettuce, tomatoes, mayonnaise, and some of tonight's left-over roast beef on the table in front of him. Big deduction—we'd surprised him in the act of making a sandwich.

"Cole slaw is good on that, too," I said.

"What?"

"On a roast-beef sandwich. Cole slaw instead of the lettuce and mayonnaise. Agnes makes a good cole slaw. There might be some left."

"Shut up. What's the girl doing here?"

"My name's Roxanne," Roxanne said. "Hi, Barry."

"Don't 'Hi' me. What are you doing with this—this—"

He couldn't think of anything bad enough to call me. After a few more thises, Roxanne came to my rescue.

"The same as you," she said. "I got a little hungry, and I asked Matt to come down with me while I raided the icebox."

He narrowed his eyes at her. "You may lose your appetite after I blow his guts all over the kitchen."

I got a mental picture of that, and I'll admit, it did a hell of a job on *my* appetite.

"May I put my hands down?"

"No. Who knows what you could be hiding in that sweat suit?"

I knew I should have worn the shorts. "Then, may I ask you a question?"

"Make it fast."

"Why are you so sure I killed your father?"

"I *heard* the two of you together. I heard him talking to you."

"What did we say?"

Barry looked sullen. "I couldn't make out all the words."

143

"What did I say?"

"I couldn't make out anything you said. You were whispering or mumbling or something."

The shotgun made a big difference. If it weren't for the shotgun, I would have laughed or shaken my head or both. I was learning, though, that no matter how silly he's being, a man with a shotgun commands respect.

"Then how did you know it was me with him?" I asked respectfully.

"What are you trying to pull?" Barry demanded.

It's very had to be persuasive with your hands up, but I did my best. "I'm not trying to pull anything. We've got a serious misunderstanding going on here, and I want to work it out."

"You're trying to trick me."

"I'm not trying to trick you. If it made any difference, I'd give you my solemn word of honor that I was *not* with your father last night."

"Ha!"

"Exactly. If you think I'm a killer, then my word doesn't mean much. I'm trying to see if there's something logical that would convince you I'm telling the truth." I was also trying to get him to lower that shotgun before I shit my pants, but it wasn't a good idea to tell him that.

Barry laughed and shook his head at me. You can do that when you're the one with the shotgun. "You can't logic your way out of this one, Cobb. *My father called you by name!*"

"Oh, Christ," I said.

Barry didn't hear the disgust in my voice. "Is that supposed to be a prayer?" he sneered. He took a tighter grip on the shotgun.

I could feel little tributaries of sweat merging to form a cold river down my back. "Barry," I said as calmly as I could, "has it occurred to you that your father might have been talking *about* me?"

"About you?"

"Why not? He'd offered me a job, already." A touchy subject, but this had to make so much sense, even a paranoid like Barry Dost would understand it. "He'd offered me a job, and he was also probably trying to figure out what the Network had in mind sending me here."

"He already knew," Barry said. His hands were looser on the gun. "He knew everything about you Network people."

"All right, he knew. Then he could have been filling someone in. Or giving him—"

"Or her," Barry said portentously. I was beginning to get the feeling I'd get out of this alive.

I nodded enthusiastically. "Or her. Giving whoever it was his impressions of the talks, now that he'd met all of us Network people face-to-face."

Barry frowned. "Talking about you," he said.

"A person's name comes up when you talk about him more than when you're talking to him," I said.

"Sure," Roxanne chipped in. "You should have heard how many times *your* name came up today."

"Sure." His voice was bitter. "Everybody trying to say I killed my father." The shotgun came up a little. If I lived, I was going to have to give Roxanne a swift kick in the ass.

"Nonono," I said. "Just wondering why you weren't there to tell your own story."

"I wanted to think."

"Think now," I told him. "I had no reason to kill your father or even hurt him. You may know something that can help pin the murder on the real killer. Come and talk to the others."

He was thinking it over. He didn't like it much, but apparently life as the castle ghost had lost its appeal for him.

"It's too late to wake the others," he said. "Let's make some sandwiches." He turned away and leaned the shotgun up against the sink. It wasn't the greatest gun safety

I'd ever heard of—in fact, it stank—but I wasn't going to worry about it. Now that he'd put the gun down, I controlled the situation, thanks to Spot. The Samoyed could make a meal of the guy before he ever got anywhere close to the weapon.

Roxanne and I sat down at the table. Roxanne grabbed a knife and started cutting a tomato into neat, round slices.

"Tell you why I decided to trust you," Barry said.

"Pass the bread," Roxanne said.

"I'd like to know."

"It was her. Roxanne. She was being so afraid for you, and so brave. And she isn't the type of woman who'd let a man fool her."

"Just once," Roxanne said. "And I used that one up long ago. Meat, please?"

It seemed to me his logic in trusting me was as faulty as it had been in suspecting me. Maybe Bats's prediction had already come through, and Barry had already gone off the deep end.

"Who could—" I was distracted for a second by Roxanne. If the size of her hunger reflected the intensity of her love, I was one lucky man. She'd built a sandwich the size of a manhole cover; she took a bite out of it that would have made a shark's mother tell it it was bolting its food. She saw me looking at her, and shrugged. At least I wasn't going to have to teach her not to talk with her mouth full.

I turned back to Barry. "Who do you think your father might have been talking to about me?"

"I don't know." He thought for a second, then said it again. "It wouldn't be Norman or his wife. If it was Uncle Jack or Aranda, why would they deny it?"

"Nobody likes to be the last known person to see the victim alive, because people have this irritating tendency to assume you're the murderer."

"The way I did with you."

"Exactly. So if it wasn't me, and it wasn't Jack or Aranda, who was it?"

"I don't know," Barry said again. He sounded irritable. "The lawyers didn't show up because of the snow, those two and me are the only people he might have been talking to confidentially in the middle of the night."

"I think you're being a little naive, Barry."

"What do you mean?"

"Your father was famous for playing all the angles. Doesn't he have somebody inside the Network?"

"What? Oh. Sure he does. Did. Of course he did."

"Who? Could it have been somebody here for the negotiations?"

"Oh, my God, it could." Barry clapped a hand to his head as if to hold the top of his skull in place. "Cobb, you're right, I never should have run away. If we'd had a chance to talk about this earlier . . ."

"It's okay," I said.

"Anybody want a soda?" Roxanne asked.

"Coke," I said. What the hell, I thought. I wasn't going to get any sleep, anyway. Barry asked for one, too.

"Somebody from the Network's been tipping off my father, and gets cold feet, who knows why? And decided he has to kill him."

"Yeah. The big question," I said, "is who?"

"I don't know. I don't know. Dad never told me things like that. And I've been busy with all this PR stuff, working on the image, you know, I wouldn't have had time to ask even if I thought he would tell me."

"That," I said, "is a shame."

"It sure is. You'll have to ask Jack, or even Aranda. She's taken a big interest in these proceedings for some reason."

"She says it's because she used to be in show business," I told him.

Barry snorted. "Yeah, right. I think she was looking for dirt on the old man because her time was about up, and

147

she was looking for a way around that prenuptial agreement."

"What do you mean, her time was about up?"

"Little things. Dad stopped lighting her cigarettes. He stopped saying 'Your ma and I,' when Aranda wanted me to do something. He was just—pulling away. After all, I've seen it twice before. I know the signs."

That seemed very interesting, but the more I thought about it, the less it seemed to mean. As a possible motive for murder, it stank. Killing Dost certainly wouldn't help her get around any prenuptial agreement.

Now Barry put on his aggressive face. "You know," he said sternly, "I've got a question or two for you, Cobb."

"Ask."

"Do *you* have a candidate for Network spy?"

"As a matter of fact," I said, "I do."

"Who is it?"

I never had to explain why I wasn't going to tell him, because at that moment a woman's scream split the house in two.

16

It's time once again to take you . . . *one step beyond!*
—John Newland, "Alcoa Presents" (ABC)

Barry's eyes went immediately to the sink, where the shotgun was leaning. He was still looking at it as he began to get out of his chair.

I grabbed his wrist. "Leave the gun," I said.

"Are you crazy?"

"The hallway's going to be crowded up there. Leave the gun. It can cause more problems than it can solve."

He looked longingly at it.

"We're wasting time," I said.

Barry tore his eyes away. "Aaaaagh! All right, then, let's go."

"Right. Wait here, Rox," I said.

She said something around a mouthful of sandwich that was probably "Fat chance," or one of its ruder equivalents. She sure didn't wait there. It was all I could do to get through the swinging door before her.

When I got to the top of the first flight of stairs, the screams told me more. They were the screams of Aranda

Dost, they were coming from above and down the end of the hall. And they were calling my name.

"Matt! Matt Cobb! Get up here! Get up here right away!"

Roxanne said, "If that's the way women call you in the middle of the night, I'm glad I got my claim in first."

I saved my breath for climbing.

As I ran down the end of the hall, Jack Bromhead stuck his face out of his room. "Dammit, Cobb, what is it?"

"Don't know," I said, and kept running.

Behind me, I heard Bromhead cursing his ankle and saying he'd be along in a minute, as soon as he found something. Fine with me. If I was about to go face-to-face with a killer (with my newfound, thickheaded love dogging my footsteps), I wanted all the help I could get. Short of Barry Dost with a shotgun behind me, that is.

Now there was a new scare—the screaming stopped. I had to remember where Aranda's room was. She couldn't bear staying in her old one, she'd said. Right—directly above Jack's, one flight up. Next door to Barry's. It was one of the bare-bones, not-yet-decorated rooms we'd searched this morning.

Up the stairs at the end of the hall, a short way down the corridor, and there it was.

The first thing I saw was Ralph, looking like a cologne ad in his uncle's pajama bottoms and hairy chest, standing in the open door of the room. He was lit by something from within the room that flickered like blue firelight. I knew that kind of light. I spent a large portion of my life bathed in it. It was the light of a TV set.

I was getting good and sick of running up and down those stairs. It took my last breath to say Ralph's name.

"Cobb!" he said. "Get in here."

"Wh—Wha—"

"I don't *know* what it is. You just see for yourself."

I shrugged, and stepped through the door. Aranda Dost sat up on her bed, dressed in a sheer black thing that had ridden up her legs and down her bosom because she was making tight fists in the material. Her eyes were wide, and her mouth was open. She was breathing, "No. No. No." Her gaze was fixed on the TV screen.

I couldn't blame her. The face on the screen was that of G. B. Dost, the late business tycoon.

Dost was standing in front of a plain black background. He wore a gray business suit, a white shirt, and a red tie. He was talking.

"What's taking you so long?" the TV said. *"Barry, are you there? Why'd you want to put an old man through this?"*

It's a tape, I thought. Then I remembered. This room hadn't been fixed up. I walked to the TV set. The phantom Dost kept expressing his impatience.

Aranda finally deigned to notice me. "Where are your wiseass remarks now, Mr. Cobb?" she spat. "You wanted a sign? How's *this* for a sign? Oh, Gabriel, it's all right, Darling. We'll get you safely across, and we'll find out what happened to you—"

I tuned her out and looked at the back of the TV set. I looked at the input jack—nothing. I looked at the antenna terminals—nothing. I followed the power cord to the outlet of the wall. I pulled the plug.

The screen went dark—the room went black. Well, he couldn't bring electricity from beyond the grave, at least.

"For God's sake, Cobb, what are you doing?" Haskell Freed's voice. I looked at the doorway. The whole gang was there, jockeying for position and asking each other what was going on.

I put the plug back in. Gabby Dost flickered across the darkness again.

"Dammit, Barry, it's hotter than hell in here."

Aranda Dost let loose a sound that combined the most poignant features of a sob and a gasp.

The set was tuned to Channel 4. I pushed the button for Channel 5 and got nothing. I pushed Channel 3 and got,

151

you should pardon the expression, a ghost. I went back to Channel 4.

"Where the hell are you, boy?" the TV demanded.

And suddenly, there he was, in the doorway. He'd elbowed his way through the crowd and was staring at the TV set. I had never seen such rage on a human face. Aranda looked at him and turned so white it was apparent even in the dim light of the TV set.

It was justified, since most of Barry's hate and rage seemed to be directed at her. If he'd had the shotgun with him, Aranda, and anybody who might have tried to stand between him and Aranda, would have been blasted to hamburger.

As it was, he went for her with his bare hands, diving for the bed, snarling, "You lying bitch."

He didn't make it. Ralph, assisted by Calvin Gowe, getting involved for once, wrapped him up and dragged him out into the hall. Barry was not quite frothing at the mouth, but he seemed to be just a few seconds away from it.

On the screen, Gabby Dost was scratching his head irritably. "Barry?" he said. "Barry?"

The picture broke up; the screen showed an electronic blizzard, and the stereo speakers produced a raucus howl. Exactly, I thought, what a TV set in a remote rural area, miles away from any transmissions, not hooked up to an antenna or cable, could be *expected* to be doing.

But I was disappointed. There hadn't been much in the way of set or script to the Gabby Dost show, but it held my attention. I tried the other channels, all eighty-two of them. All I found on them was more snow, and we'd had enough of that this week, already.

"Turn on the light," I said. Aranda was sitting as if in a trance. "Aranda!"

"Did you see?" she demanded. "Did you *see*?"

"I saw. Turn on the light, okay?"

As soon as she did, I turned off the TV. "Okay," I began.

There was another scream, a man's this time, from out in the hallway. I dove through the throng to see Calvin Gowe bent over Ralph Ingersoll, whose nose was showering blood on the hall carpet. Barry, once again, was scampering down the corridor.

"The little bastard head-butted him," Gowe said.

"Brote by dose," Ralph contributed.

That much was obvious. I'd save my sympathy for later. "Roxanne," I called, and she appeared like a genie from a bottle. "Take care of Ralph. Cal, you go in that room and see that nobody touches that TV set."

Cal grinned slightly, no doubt at the possibility that he'd be able to hit somebody in the near future.

Roxanne had knelt beside Ralph and was asking him if he could breathe all right. She looked up at me. "And you, I suppose, are going to try to keep Barry from disappearing again."

I nodded and took off. In fact, I didn't think he was going to disappear this time. I figured I knew exactly where he was going.

He was going to the kitchen to get that shotgun that was leaning against the sink.

I didn't take off in Barry's tracks, figuring that if he heard me behind him, he'd just increase his speed. Also, the side stairs were a slightly shorter route to the kitchen, and I might be able to head him off at the sink.

This route took me once again past Jack Bromhead's room.

Jack's voice rang out, filled with effort and impatience. "What the hell is going on out there?"

"No time!" I yelled back, and kept running. I hit the main hall, turned and sprinted for the kitchen. No sign of Barry. About ten feet from the swinging door, I put my arm out like Walter Payton, getting ready to stiff-arm the door out of the way.

There is a bit that recurs in a number of Bugs Bunny cartoons, wherein Bugs is blithely doing something incredibly stupid, then realizes it. He looks at the audience and screams, "WHAT AM I DOING?"

That's what happened to me. My feet did not actually leave skid marks on the floor as I screeched to a stop, but I wouldn't have been surprised if they had.

I was right to stop. The door swung open, and there was Barry Dost, shotgun at the ready, trigger finger at the ready, to blow somebody away. His face told me his heart and mind were ready, too.

"Don't move," he said.

Since I was already frozen solid, this was an easy order to follow. I wondered idly if my bowels counted.

"Get out of my way," Barry ordered.

"Uh—I—uh have to move to do that, Barry."

"Don't you use my name. I almost *trusted* you. But you're in it with them, aren't you? *Aren't you?*"

"I'm not in anything with anybody," I said.

He wasn't paying attention to me. "How stupid can you get?" he asked the world at large, which at this point consisted mostly of himself. "I showed them. I fucking *showed* them.

"And you helped!" I was back in his world again. "Getting me there, so—"

He lifted the shotgun to his shoulder. If he'd shot from the hip, he would have cut me in half. He couldn't have missed at that range. But Barry had apparently been taken bird hunting and taught how to use a shotgun, so he took a split second to raise the thing to his shoulder and aim.

In that split second, a voice behind me said, "Cobb! Down!"

I dropped. Gunshots rang out behind me. Barry staggered back, fired the shotgun into the ceiling, and fell.

I took a breath, then turned around to see Jack Bromhead, in an ancient purple bathrobe, limping down the hallway carrying a silvery Colt .45 revolver, the Gun That Won the West.

"You okay?"

"Yeah," I said. "Thanks." I walked over to Barry Dost. I was careful, even though I could see the glassy eyes and the two holes in the middle of the chest. I kicked the shotgun out of reach. As I did, I thought of something we should have done as soon as there was any evidence of foul play. We should have put a lock on the gun-room door.

17

I'm going to take you apart like a clock.
—William Conrad, "Jake and the Fatman" (CBS)

My hands were shaking as I undid the last screw.

I admit it might have been nerves—being that close to the receiving end of a shotgun blast isn't an experience I'm eager to repeat. I wasn't crazy about watching Barry Dost breathe his last, either, but since it had come down to him or me, I'm just as glad it was him.

"What's the matter, boy?" Jack Bromhead asked.

Jack was lying on the bed recently occupied by Aranda Dost, his bad foot propped up on a pillow. Aranda had been led back to her old room, in the suite she'd shared with her husband. After what had happened tonight, she'd decided she could face it after all.

"Nothing," I lied. I took a deep breath and put the screwdriver in the screw head again.

My hands still wanted to shake, but I wouldn't let them. I decided I hoped it *was* nerves. I really and truly hoped my hands weren't shaking because I was afraid of what I might find inside this TV set. Or rather, of what I might not find.

Things would have been better if I'd been able to tackle the TV set as soon as the lead stopped flying, when the adrenaline of near death would have carried me through without giving me time to think too much. Unfortunately, of all the millions of things G. B. Dost had owned, the thousands of them under the gabled roof of Rocky Point, the hardest one to find was a Phillips screwdriver.

A lot of things had happened while Fred Norman and Cal Gowe scoured the house for the necessary tool. Aranda Dost had been led away, alternately muttering and screaming at me that she had told me not to scoff at what I didn't understand. Barry Dost had been deposited in the outdoor deep freeze alongside his father. Roxanne, who along with countless academic degrees had somewhere picked up an expert knowledge of first aid, had taken charge of Ralph Ingersoll's nose. Ralph was sleeping now, courtesy of some of Jack Bromhead's codeine tablets.

"Where the hell do you get all this codeine?" I asked in an idle moment. "Did Dost own a pharmaceutical company or something?"

"No, but he owns—owned—the biggest distributor— legal distributor—in the Pacific Northwest. Which, with gas prices back up, has been giving us a royal pain, to tell you the truth."

He laughed. "Drugs, giving us a pain. It's supposed to be the other way around. Anyway, that doesn't have anything to do with it. This stuff is all legal. This isn't the first time this place has ever been snowbound, you know."

"Just the worst."

"You got that right. But with the place being inaccessible sometimes, and folks skiing, and doing other foolish things"—he pointed at his own sprained ankle—"we knew we'd have to be set up better than just having a first-aid kit around. So we got a local doctor to prescribe everything we might need for us to take care of an emergency, ourselves. We all had to go through first-aid training, too, though I don't think I'd be as good as that Schick gal."

I got the screw out at last. It felt hot in my hand. I put it in my pocket, and reached to remove the black plastic back of the set.

"Wait a minute," Jack Bromhead said. "Don't do that yet. You probably want another witness."

"What's wrong with you?"

"What's wrong with me is that I'm counting on you to be *my* witness about shooting poor Barry. If you're my only witness for that, and I'm your only witness for what's inside this TV set, it might wind up looking to the authorities like a real case of logrolling."

He had a point. I supposed I ought to get one of the Network people in here. I stuck my head out into the hallway. Bats Blefary and Carol Coretti had been keeping lookout. Actually, Bats had been flirting with Carol, and she had been being civil back. I would, I decided, be doing Bats a favor by interrupting things.

I called them over.

Bats had thrown on jeans and a T-shirt. Carol was wearing the same outfit she'd worn last night. This thing was turning into one long, horrifying pajama party.

"What's up, Matt?" Bats wanted to know.

I looked at him and Carol. "Did you both see what was on this screen earlier tonight . . . I mean, this morning?"

"Please, Matt," Carol said. "Stick with tonight, or you'll confuse me terribly. I wasn't asleep long enough for it to be tomorrow yet. But yes, I saw it."

"What did you think?"

"Videotape," Bats said. "I wondered what all the screaming was about."

"But then you found out there was no input hooked up to the set," Carol said. "I didn't know what to think."

"Wait a minute," Jack Bromhead said. "Cobb, I thought

you were fixing to explain how it was done. Maybe even do it again. I didn't get to see it, first time around."

"I'm fixing to do just that. I hope."

"Well, get on with it."

"Okay. You suggested more witnesses. I'm just bringing them—and you—up to speed on my thinking."

Jack Bromhead laughed. "Hell, after what you been through tonight, I'm surprised you can be thinking anything."

I looked at him. "I don't want to sound ungrateful or anything, but for someone who's just recently blown away somebody who called you 'Uncle Jack,' you seem pretty chipper yourself."

Jack Bromhead gave me a look that made me glad the Colt was out of reach. Then his face softened. "The place and time I grew up, men were taught not to show if they were hurting. Shake it off, shrug it off, laugh it off. Get on with it. It might not be the way to be, but it's the only way I know. But don't think I ain't busted up inside. I played cowboys with Barry when he could hardly walk. He was a good boy. It was just that as a man he couldn't . . . I don't know, he just couldn't make the pieces fit. He was off the deep end, and he probably killed his daddy, and for sure he was gonna kill you. So I did what I had to do, all right?"

Jack clapped his hands together sharply. I jumped. So did Bats and Carol.

"All right!" he said. "Educate this ignorant old man. What were you saying?"

"My first thought was videotape, too. The fact that Dost's picture only came in on Channel 4, with a subimage on Channel 3, was suggestive."

"Why?"

"Because videotape players in this country are built to send their output through Channel 3 or Channel 4. Look at any of them, you'll find a switch. You just pick the one in your area that doesn't have a broadcasting station on it, and let it go."

"What difference does a broadcasting station make?" Carol wanted to know. I was embarrassed for her for a second, until I remembered that she was a lawyer who happened to work for the Network, not a broadcasting person.

"Interference," Bats said.

"Right. In principle, a VCR *is* a broadcast station, in miniature. It feeds the same kind of signals, and your TV interprets them the same way it interprets what it gets over the air, or from a cable system. In fact, you run the cable from the machine to the TV; you've set up your own mini cable system."

"Okay, I follow you. If you've got some Channel 3 coming into your TV set from the air, you don't want to fight it with your machine."

"Right. Which is exactly the case here. So you set your VCR to Channel 4."

"But there *was* no VCR," Carol insisted. "You established that yourself."

"Not quite," I told her. "What I established was that there was no tape being fed into the TV *from the outside*."

"Ahh," Jack Bromhead said. "And that's why you—"

"That's why I've unscrewed the back. I want to see what there is on the *inside*."

"A VCR wouldn't fit in there," Bats said. "*Mine* sure wouldn't."

"They come a lot smaller than yours," I said. "What have you got, a VHS? I thought so. Beta is smaller than that, eight millimeter smaller still. All we'd need is a play deck, maybe the size of a kid's lunch box."

"Even so," Carol said.

"These are big TV sets," I went on. "The size is dictated by the picture tube, which is not only big, but oddly shaped. The transistors don't take up much room at all. Most of the inside of a TV set is empty space."

I grabbed the black plastic again. "So," I said. "Let's just see." I rocked it a little to get it out of the groove it sat in, then pulled it away.

And inside, there it was. The picture tube. A few micro-circuits.

And empty space.

A whole lot of empty space. No VCR. Nothing.

I sat there looking at it. I spun the set around so everyone could see.

Jack Bromhead broke the silence. "I guess we owe Aranda an apology, boy."

I only knew I could move my lips because I heard myself talking. "Yeah. I guess so."

Bats had the TV set now. He was waving his hand around inside the thing as though the VCR were in there, invisible, and he was going to find it by touch.

"What happens now?" Carol asked.

"We go to bed and try to sleep. Tackle this again in the morning." I turned to Jack Bromhead. "Come on, Bats and I will help you back to your room."

"Nah," he said. "My damn ankle's had enough of going up and down these stairs, with or without help."

Carol was shocked. "You're going to stay here?"

"Sure. Maybe I'll even leave on the TV. Maybe Gabby will come back again, tell me what the hell to do about PharmaKing."

We left the room with the sound of Jack's not-quite-healthy laughter behind us.

18

"If" is a very special word.
—Judy Graubart, "The Electric Company" (PBS)

I shuddered as Roxanne and I walked through the downstairs hallway on the way to breakfast. Fred Norman had cleaned up the blood, but there was nothing he could have done about the shotgun blast in the ceiling. I looked at it, deliberately. I knew I was in for a long series of dreams in which I failed to stop myself outside the kitchen door, or Jack Bromhead didn't show up in time, and I figured I might as well give my subconscious accurate details to work with.

We learned at table that Aranda Dost had prepared breakfast this morning (scrambled eggs, grilled ham, biscuits) with her own soft hands, Agnes Norman being too broken up over the death of Mr. Barry to cook.

"The Normans have given notice," she said, sadly. "If it turns out to be up to me, I think I'd close this place up."

"Not sell it?" Haskell Freed asked. He punctuated the question by putting a big yellow wad of egg in his mouth.

"Oh, no," Aranda said. "Not until I'm absolutely sure Gabriel is at rest."

Ralph Ingersoll said, "How could it possibly be up to you?" He sounded irritable, and I couldn't blame him. He had a bandage strapped over his nose and two black eyes. He was facing the prospect of plastic surgery when (if?) we finally got out of here. And he still didn't have any idea what the hell was going on.

"The prenuptial agreement, and all that," Ralph went on.

Aranda didn't look at him; she seemed to be involved in stirring her coffee.

"I think it's quite possible," Wilberforce said, "that Mrs. Dost might have quite a bit to say about the disposition of the late Mr. Dost's property."

Ralph said, "How?"

"Well, estate law is not my field," he said.

"Nor mine, unfortunately," Carol Coretti put in.

"But," Wilberforce went on, "there are some interesting possibilities. In some states, such as Connecticut, where I reside, prenuptial agreements are recognized only in cases of divorce, not survivorship. A widow *must* get one third of her late husband's net worth. But that can vary by state."

"We weren't married in Connecticut, anyway," Aranda said. I tried to hear something wistful in her tone, but didn't.

"Well, one possibility is that if, as seems likely now, young Dost killed his father, he would be ineligible to take possession of his legacy. And, of course, he couldn't pass it on in turn. As far as I know—and as you must know, the Network researched Mr. Dost, and those associated with him, very thoroughly—he has no other surviving relatives. Is that correct, Mr. Bromhead?"

Jack was still looking chipper this morning. He said his foot was a lot better, too.

"No," he said. "Nobody. He had a cousin, lived like a hermit raising sheep in Montana, died in '77. That was it."

"Then the judge might rule that, agreement or no, Mrs. Dost is the only eligible heir to the estate."

"No," Aranda said. "Oh, no."

Wilberforce smiled. He doesn't have a charming smile. If a shark smiled, it would look like Charles Wilberforce. Aranda drew back visibly from him.

"I think it's quite possible, Mrs. Dost," he said. "Though, as I say, I'm not an expert."

Carol Coretti had been listening with her finger on her chin, looking thoughtful. Now she brightened. "There's something else," she said.

"Yes?" Wilberforce asked.

"Did Barry Dost leave a will? Does *he* have any living relatives?"

"Ahh," Wilberforce said. He sounded like a man who's just spotted the quotation in a Double-Crostic. A lot of lawyers are like that. Life is a game; the law is the rules; and they get to find loopholes and raise "interesting points." That's what Wilberforce said now, "Interesting point." I don't think it crossed his mind for a second that the woman's husband and stepson were actually *dead*, laid out like a couple of mackerel in a fish store in the chill of the shed in back.

"What's the interesting point?" Jack Bromhead wanted to know.

Carol Coretti deferred to her boss. "Well, Mr. Bromhead, suppose Barry Dost did *not* murder his father? Then the estate would pass through him, minus other bequests, of course. But now he's dead, too. If he died intestate, and has no other relatives . . ."

"He doesn't. His ma was the last of her line, too."

"Then it's very likely a court would declare Mrs. Dost Barry's next of kin, and she'd inherit the estate that way."

"I don't care to talk about it anymore. Right now, I don't care what happens to the money. I just want to get out of here and start putting my life back together."

"So do we all." Haskell Freed's voice was hearty. "You know, I wonder what's taking them so long. You'd think at least the telephone service would be back."

Yeah, I thought, you would if you didn't know the phone console had been smashed. That was a little mystery our supernatural visitation had failed to clean up. I decided to let the phone company go on taking the rap until I thought of something, or until we were rescued. Of course, in order to be rescued, someone's got to suspect you're in trouble. As far as I could tell, nobody did.

Aranda wanted to talk about a different kind of communication.

"You saw it, Mr. Cobb," she said. "You were there and you saw it. Gabriel delayed his Crossing to help you solve the case."

"I certainly saw what there was to see, Mrs. Dost."

"You can't still be skeptical! If it wasn't a Visit, what was it?"

"I am fully prepared to admit I saw something last night I can't explain."

She smiled at me, not quite gloating. "Jack told me about your searching the inside of the TV set."

"Well," I said. "We don't want to leave any loopholes for future skeptics, do we?"

"Future skeptics?"

"Of course. This is going to be a sensation when we tell the story. The first mysterious death. Barry's disappearance. Your husband's voice from the Other Side. Jack's heroics. I'm predicting no fewer than six books about it."

"People can be such vultures," she said. She didn't look especially horrified, however.

"That's why we're lucky to have had this happen in front of so many unimpeachable witnesses. And no one had the chance to remove anything from the TV set before I checked it. So our story will stand up to scrutiny, which is sure to come." I sighed. "Still, I think some people will never believe us. They'll turn themselves inside out trying to come up with theories that would explain all of us being in a conspiracy to get away with murder."

"Nonsense!" Wilberforce huffed.

"Think about it, Charles," I said.

"I—I don't believe in the supernatural, but I saw what I saw."

"Then you *must* come to believe in the supernatural," Aranda said gently. "How can you doubt the evidence of your own senses and reason?"

Wilberforce subsided, muttering into his napkin.

"How did you come to turn on the TV last night, Mrs. Dost?" I asked.

She turned to me. "Excuse me?"

"I was wondering why you turned on the television in that room. You must have known it wasn't hooked up. Were you *expecting* something out of the ordinary to happen?"

She smiled. "Oh, no. I was simply so tired, I didn't really know what I was doing. Force of habit—I watch TV on most nights before I go to sleep. It relaxes me."

She tilted her head to the side and put a finger to her chin. "Of course, it's *possible* . . ."

"Yes?"

"It's just *possible* that my actions were channeled. That Gabriel was guiding my actions so that he could help me resolve my turmoil."

"Uh-huh. That makes sense. I also think it's interesting that out of the eighty-three channels the set can receive, Mr. Dost's spirit came in on the same one that the cable and VCR signals would come into."

That, it seemed, was funny enough to make her laugh. "Mr. Cobb, that's the simplest thing of all!"

"How so?"

"That channel is where we'd *expect* to find a show.

Gabriel's business last night was to communicate a terrible truth. He wanted to make sure the message got across."

"Which it did. Thanks to you."

"I was the closest to him," she said softly. "Another factor is that the TV would be *ready* to receive on Channel 4. That's the way things happen all the time—the house's aura would have preconditioned the TV to work best that way. Don't you see?"

An honest answer would have been, "Huh?" But I just nodded.

"Well, there you have it. It's not *easy* for someone to cross back from the Other Side, you know."

"I wouldn't think so," I said. "It happens so seldom."

"Oh, more than you think. The point is, these things happen efficiently, or not at all. And now, if you'll all excuse me? I'd like to be alone for a while."

So, for the second morning in a row, she walked out on us. Today, though, she seemed as happy as any woman twice recently bereaved had any right to be.

19

"If we ever get out of here," Ralph Ingersoll told me, "I'm going to college to become an accountant."

I played straight for him. "Why's that, Ralph?"

"Because accountants don't get their goddam noses broken." He brought his left hand up to the bandage and touched it gingerly. He hissed in pain and drew his hand down to his lap.

We were up in Ralph's room. He sat in one of the wooden-armed hotel chairs with his feet up on his bed. He said it hurt too much when he was lying down. I sat in another of the chairs, looking at the patterns the pale but determined winter sun made on the floor.

"Maybe it would be better if you stopped touching it," I suggested.

Ralph groaned. "The only thing that hurts worse than touching it is not touching it."

"Pills working?"

"I hope not," he said. "If they are, I can just imagine what this is going to feel like when they wear off."

"Can I do anything?"

"Can you get me to a real doctor?"

"Not right now."

"Do you believe in mercy killing?"

"No."

"Then you can't do anything for me." He raised his head, then thought better of it. "Goddammit," he said. "All that football, never so much as jock itch. And now this."

"And now what?" I asked him. "Football left you unscathed, so a simple thing like a murder case should be taken in stride? That's the thing about murder cases, Ralph. People get hurt."

"That's why I'm gonna be an accountant. Since Barry mashed my face, I've been thinking that being a deputy sheriff, no matter how bogus, and spending my life on the road in a big clunky limousine are both too high-risk for me."

"Want to come work for the Network?"

Ralph said, "Ha," a couple of times, then groaned. "Don't make me laugh, it hurts. With Dost dead, who knows what the hell is going to happen to your Network?"

"It'll survive. The stock will go down, so what? The Network will still make shows, the advertisers will still pay for them, and people will still watch."

"And Matt Cobb will still come within an inch of being shotgunned into Gaines Burgers."

"The Network hires accountants, too."

"I'll keep it in mind," Ralph said. "Now, what the hell do you want from me?"

"I think we should take the wraps off them. That you should. You're in charge here, after all."

He'd been touching the bandage as I said it. Now he hissed, laughed and groaned all at once. "I told you not to make me laugh. What do you mean, take the wraps off?"

"I mean, let them run around loose. Go skiing if they want to. Forget this three-at-a-time business. Just generally act as though we believe Barry killed Dost, Dost fingered Barry, and Bromhead shot a homicidally loony Barry. Case closed."

"Are you serious?" Pain or no pain, Ralph leaned forward to look at me.

"I'm serious that that's what I want you to do."

"I mean, do you seriously believe there was a haunted TV set here cracking the case for you last night?"

"I seriously believe I can't explain it. I said that at breakfast."

"I know. I heard you. I thought you were up to something clever. Listen, Cobb, I can't explain what makes my Aunt Agnes's bread rise, either. That doesn't mean I have to believe little bread pixies blow it up like a balloon."

"No," I said, "you don't. But if you couldn't have any bread unless you said you believed in the pixies, what harm would it do?"

"You lost me."

"I think there's someone who would like us to believe very much that Barry killed Dost, and that Barry's death brings things to a close. With or without the intervention of the supernatural. And I think we'll all be a lot safer if this person thinks we've bought it."

"Ah," Ralph said. "We let him *think* we've bought it. What do we do in the meantime? Not that I'm going to be much good for anything, mind you. Just that if I'm supposed to be in charge here, I probably ought to know what's going on."

"Come on," I said. "If Jack Bromhead can limp around playing cavalry with a sprained ankle, you can still be in charge with a broken nose."

"That's what I need, a pep talk. What are we going to do?"

"I don't know."

"Well, I'm with you, so far."

"You're getting good at this banter stuff," I told him.

"Let's just say that my turmoil takes a whole lot more resolving than Aranda's does."

"You don't buy the message from the Other Side?"

"Even if I did, I wouldn't be satisfied with it. I mean, I know it's rude. I know the guy came back from the dead for me and all, but the way I see it, what's the point of resurrecting yourself if you're going to leave so many questions?"

"Like, why did Barry kill you in the first place?"

"That's the simplest of all, as our hostess would say. Barry was 'unstable.' So he did 'unstable' things. I had in mind questions more along the line of, how did your body get so far from the house without leaving any marks?"

Ralph opened his eyes wide. They showed very white against the background of black and blue. "My God. I'd forgotten all about that, can you believe it? I guess my brain can only handle one impossible thing at a time."

"It's not the impossible that bothers me."

"You sure *acted* bothered."

"Okay, it bothers me. But it's a *trick*. The impossible stuff in this case doesn't bother me nearly so much as the unfathomable stuff."

"Like?"

"Like why was the phone smashed? That, more than anything, was what made me think we were locked in with some maniac who was going to try to pick us off one by one. I couldn't think of another reason for us to be so vehemently cut off from the outside world."

"We've only been here a couple of days, Cobb."

"And we'll only be here a couple more."

"Oh? Did you get a message from the National Guard or something?"

"No, I got a message from The Weather Channel. Strong winds tonight as a warm front moves through. Heavy rain tomorrow, followed by unseasonably high temperature, perhaps into the fifties."

"Yeah. That happens once a winter. We call it the January thaw."

"This is February."

Ralph shrugged. "Maybe it forgot. In any case a lot of snow will melt. And wait till you see the mud."

"All I want to see is the cops. But let's get back to the point. Can you think of a reason for the phone to be cut off?"

"Not really."

"Work on it. I will, too."

Ralph said he would. "Any more unfa— What was that?"

"Unfathomables. Yeah. The biggie. What the hell is going on with Aranda Dost and Carol Coretti?"

"I thought nothing was going on. Coretti is a happily married whatever working for your Network, and you trusted her implicitly."

"Yeah. But none of it makes sense. Carol tells me Aranda made a pass at her. Aranda denies it. She not only denies it, she swears that if she'd known Carol was a lesbian, she would never have let her in the house."

"That's an old-fashioned attitude, but a lot of people still have it," Ralph said. "So what?"

"So it's a great big lie," I said. "What have we been hearing since we got here? Gabby Dost, dealmaker of dealmakers, the slickest of the slick. Finds out everything findable about the people he'll be dealing with. Has to know what makes them tick. The whole gang has been throwing little facts of *my* life at me since I got here.

"Furthermore, we've had the tale of Aranda's great interest in the purchase of the Network. Whether because she wanted to start singing again, or because she wanted a channel for her channeler, as it were, or if she was just interested because it's show biz doesn't matter. Everybody, including Aranda herself, has been telling us how she's been kept up to speed on this whole deal.

"But she didn't know Carol Coretti is gay. I wouldn't buy that for a bent nickel."

"Neither would I, once you line it out like that." Ralph raised his arm high in the air to look at his watch. "Damn," he said. "Still another hour before I can take my medicine. Keep talking. You take my mind off my troubles."

"I had no intention of stopping," I told him. "Now, try to figure out why Aranda lied about that part of it at all. It was a dumb lie, the kind I was bound to catch."

"Maybe she was ashamed of wanting to take a fling with a dyke on the night her husband was killed. Maybe she was panic-stricken and guilty. She wanted to make it seem impossible that she'd made a pass at the other woman."

"I suppose it's possible," I said. "But does Aranda strike you as the kind of woman who would stay panic-stricken for hours at a time?"

"That's another thing," Ralph said. "Accountants only have to figure out numbers. Not women."

"Still and all. This didn't happen in the craziness surrounding the finding of the body. We asked her about Carol in the calmness of the sitting room, where we'd been asking people questions all afternoon. She had plenty of time to prepare herself."

"You've got another theory, though."

"Yeah. How did you know?"

"You wouldn't have brought this all up if you didn't have one. What is it?"

"That Carol Coretti was spying for Dost at the Network. That she's been feeding them details of what the Network was going to ask for, and that's why Aranda pretended to know nothing about her."

I sighed. "Except, if that's true, why did Carol go to Wilberforce, and ultimately me, with this whole lesbian business? That only served to draw attention to her."

"So that doesn't make any sense, either."

"No," I said. "It does not. As I said, unfathomable. I wish

174

we'd had a whole lot more of the Ghost of Dost, or none at all. As it is, it's a mess. Which, I think, is the way someone wants it."

"What do you mean?"

"I don't think whoever's behind this necessarily expects us to gaze into our crystals and chant that the supernatural has solved everything for us. I think he—or she—wants to make us feel that things are so screwed up now that it's going to take the rest of our lives, and any succeeding ones, to make this make any sense, so that we'll roll over for the easy solution."

"Barry did it."

"Yeah. In a way, it's almost lucky for Barry that he's dead. It would be hard to deny an accusation from a dead man."

"Don't forget, if Bromhead hadn't gotten there in time, *you'd* be in a position to make accusations from beyond."

"I know, I know." I tried not to shudder. "Why do you keep reminding me of that?"

"Because you seem so eager to forget it. What's the point here? Are you trying to tell me you want to spend the rest of your incarnations working on this thing? I may have to, being *in charge* and all."

"No, no. I just don't want to let a murderer put one over on me without doing everything I can."

"That's the question. What can you do?"

I shrugged. "We can stir a little freedom and goodwill and fresh air into the mix and see what happens."

"You don't think anybody else is in danger?"

"No, I think everybody but me is happy with the way things are now."

"Then go tell them."

"You do it," I said. "You're in charge."

And if I hadn't ducked the ashtray he threw at me, I'd have a broken nose, too.

20

That's it! It all made sense now.
—Lorenzo Music, "Garfield's Babes and Bullets" (CBS)

It was hard to decide who was happier to be outside,
Roxanne or Spot. Roxanne was a purple streak down the
mountain in the bright sunlight. I'd already seen her come
down twice. She skidded to a stop, then slid gently over to
Spot and me.

"This is great!" she said. "You don't know what you're
missing."

I smiled at her. "Sure I do. All I have to do is watch Jack
limp and listen to Ralph groaning in pain, and I know
what I'm missing."

"Party poop," she said. "I'm in love with a party poop."

"Besides," I said. "This is the only day you'll have for
this, if the weather forecast holds up. You don't want to
waste it on the bunny slope, or whatever the hell you call
it."

"I don't care about that, so much. The weather, I mean.
It will be good to get out of here."

"As soon as the driveway is visible," I promised her.

"Okay," she said. "The mountain calls." I wouldn't have

thought she could kiss me while she was standing on skis, but she did a little dip thing with one knee and leaned sideways enough for me to bend over and meet her. Very nice. I felt like a jerk for having denied myself the pleasure for so long.

Still, everything has its price, and I was beginning to suspect the form of payment I'd have to render to Roxanne Schick. Sooner or later, my newfound beloved was going to end me up in traction by making me ski.

While I was making gloomy predictions, I also foresaw a lot of tsuris when we could finally get out of here, and Ralph and I told everyone they weren't going home, but to the sheriff's office for questioning. I wasn't expecting any actual bloodshed, but it wouldn't be pleasant. I'd like it a lot better if I could walk in there with a story that had more behind it than the one I had now. "A ghost told it to me" was good enough for Hamlet, but the State of New York is a lot more rigid about those things than the State of Denmark.

To hell with it. I decided to worry about that when the time came. I took Spot off the lead and just let him run. Samoyeds were bred to be sled dogs—running in the snow is what they like best. Spot left dog prints all over the snow we had so carefully kept unmarked. It didn't matter. The wind and the rain would do it in by tomorrow, anyway. Spot ran over and sniffed the now brownish-black hole in the snow where G. B. Dost's body had lain.

"Spot! Here, boy!"

Spot was glad to oblige. He can smell, all right, but he's no hound. He'd be curious about blood, but not obsessive.

I gave him (and me) a good, long walk. I was getting good at using snowshoes. Maybe there was hope in my learning to ski, after all.

We took one complete turn around the house. Rocky Point, up close or from a distance, was as impressive as ever. I remembered thinking when I'd first seen it that it

178

was a house built to be haunted, but I hadn't meant it so literally.

Then I remembered the note, the note that had gotten me here in the first place. The one that had warned of insanity, treachery, and murder, and I knew—*knew*, not just suspected—that someone had been leading us around by the nose up here, that what had happened had been planned.

The promise of the note had been redeemed too well for it to have been the work of a crank. I'd sooner believe in a haunted television set than that some maniac could predict so nicely what would happen in the first forty-eight hours of the Network's face-to-face acquaintance with Mr. G. B. Dost.

And speak of the poor devil, Spot and I were walking past the locked door of the shed that held the end of the Dost line just as I thought the man's name. It was the first time I'd been out here since Ralph and I had deposited the billionaire's body. Barry had been brought in by Cal Gowe and Fred Norman.

Spot ran to the wall at the edge of the cliff exactly as though he planned to jump over it.

"Spot! Stop!"

Spot is well trained. He always obeys commands in proper form. That doesn't mean he has to like them, though. He stopped, but he turned around and looked hard at me. His perpetual Samoyed's grin was more a "What's with you" kind of sneer.

I'd never looked over the wall, hadn't looked at this side of the house much at all. I walked over to it. The bricks came up to my chest; there were another eight or nine inches of snow on top of that. I wondered why they'd make a wall so low until I remembered I was standing on top of at least two feet of snow.

I brushed the snow off the top of the wall. I was careful, in case there was something nasty built into the top, but I got down to the smooth concrete cap with no problems. The man who built Rocky Point must have figured, sensibly enough, that if a nine-hundred-foot climb wasn't going to discourage intruders, barbed wire or broken glass probably wouldn't, either.

I looked over the edge and was impressed. Anything that went over this wall would fall a long way before it hit anything. It wouldn't fall all nine hundred feet, though. The rock wall angled out just a bit, with outcroppings of rock scattered more or less regularly along the wall like teeth on a grater.

I have too much imagination. I shuddered and turned away.

Spot was barking at me. He wanted to romp in the snow, and I'd made him sit in one place all this time.

I walked away from the wall, then told him he could come to me. We walked around the rest of the house. If there was anything worth noticing there, I missed it.

This route took us by the northwest corner, just below the room where all the wires came into the house. If I stood under the wires, I could look in a straight line from the house to the tall pine tree about twenty-five feet from the house, to the spot where some force had slammed G. B. Dost's body into the black teeth of the driveway rocks.

Since I had decided that I no longer gave a damn about the snow, anyway, I decided to walk that line. I wasn't looking for anything, except maybe inspiration. I remembered from junior high that any two points determined a line, and any line can be extended indefinitely. Fine. I had point A (where the body was found) and point B (that corner of the house) because not only had that room afforded the best look at Dost *in situ*, but because it was where I'd tangled with Barry that morning. The fact that the tree came smack in the middle of them had to be a coincidence. I mean, the tree was there long before the house was, long enough for the scars of lopped-off branches to have darkened to the same color as the bark.

Still, when you're faced with incredible flying corpses and haunted TV sets, you might as well check the sincerity of fine towering trees, too. I walked.

And son of a gun, it turned out that the tree wasn't *quite* on a direct line from the spot where Dost's body had been found. The tree had about a six-foot clearance to my left, maybe five. It was still plenty of room for Spot to walk alongside me, neither brushing the tree nor crowding my snowshoes. So much for The Sinister Tree Scenario, I thought.

The only wood my path took me in contact with was the skinny broken branch that had been the only thing besides the corpse that had marred the smooth whiteness of the snow the other morning. The damned thing snagged in my snowshoe, and I had a terrible time getting it out. I almost had to sacrifice my dignity and sit down in the snow, but I managed to lean against the tree and pull it loose.

I went back to the base of the lift. Fred Norman had his nose in a Thermos bottle. The grunt he made into it when he saw me might have been a sound of greeting or of disgust. I made a similar noise back.

I watched Roxanne come expertly down the last part of the hill again. Her face was very red as she slid over to us again.

"Are you that good, or is the run that easy?"

"What do you mean?"

"You never fall down."

"Cobb, you don't have to be World Class at something not to fall down while you're doing it."

"I don't know," I said. "I was second-team small college all-American basketball player, and I fell down constantly."

"That's different."

"Why?"

She stuck out her tongue and looked back up the mountain. "I'll work on it," she said.

"You do that," I said. "In the meantime, I've persuaded Spot it's time to go inside. How about you?"

"Pretty soon," she said. "I've got enough daylight for two more runs down the mountain."

"Have fun," I told her.

"I try always to have fun, whatever I'm doing. For instance, I'm going to need a hot shower when I come in in a little while. Is there any *possible* way to make a shower fun?"

"Sure," I told her. "I'll loan you my rubber duckie."

Roxanne nodded soberly. "That's a start," she said. Then she did the little kiss trick again, and went back to the chair lift.

Here we were, at the crossroads of our relationship. The woman had said she'd been carrying a torch for me since she was practically a child. Now, after one false start years ago, we'd Found Each Other. Now, on our first full day as an Item, she spends it skiing.

This was the question: Should I, or should I not, be pissed off and jealous?

I thought it over for a second. Finally I decided, nah. I was looking for a woman, a mate. An help meet for me, as the Bible would say. Not a Siamese twin.

I took Spot up to the room and fed him, then I brushed his fur so it would dry better. He loves that.

I didn't enjoy it so much. Not the work itself, which is a small price to pay to be allowed to stay in the dog's apartment back in New York, but because I couldn't stop my mind from racing.

I hate when that happens. Images, thoughts, memories, snatches of conversation start chasing each other around in my brain faster and faster until I think I'm going to go nuts. Dost dead. Barry yelling. Barry running. Barry taking the bullets. Barry dead. Aranda crying. Aranda smiling. Suspicious looks from the Normans. The view down the mountain from Rocky Point. Carol Coretti not-flirting with people. Ralph's raccoon face. Roxanne in my arms.

I tried to hold on to that last image, but the thoughts whizzed right on by. Finally, I closed my eyes and said, "Now, cut it out."

That works, for a while. The light show goes away and I walk around irritated, as though there were something itchy sitting under my brain.

Roxanne knocked—I let her in. "Spot do something?" she asked.

"No, he's been fine. I was talking to myself."

"You were very stern with yourself." She had left her parka and snow pants and skis downstairs. She was unlacing her boots.

"I deserved it," I said. "Come on, I'll show you how to have fun in the shower."

A little while later we went downstairs to the library. Roxanne felt it was the best place for aprés-ski hanging around, and I thought a change of scene might give me something else to think about. At least it might slow my brain down a little bit.

There was a fire in the library fireplace, and drink-makings and hors d'oeuvres were scattered around the place, but only Bats Blefary was taking advantage of it. He was sitting in a big leather armchair with his feet up on a matching ottoman, looking into a brandy snifter with all the intensity Aranda undoubtedly devoted to her crystals.

"Mind if we join you?" Roxanne said brightly.

Bats jumped. Not enough to spill the brandy. If I was reading the signs correctly, Bats hadn't spilled much brandy on the way to his mouth today. Not that he was drunk or anything, but his eyes had a strange glimmer, and his glasses were a little askew, and he didn't seem to care about adjusting them.

"Huh?" Bats said, looking up. "What?" Then the message sank in, and he smiled. "Oh. No. Not at all. Please, sit down."

We sat. Bats asked us what we'd been up to all afternoon. We told him. "What have you been up to?" I asked.

"Oh, just sitting here. All alone. Getting blotto on this brandy." He took a sip. "This is very, very good stuff. I'm not usually a brandy man, but Mrs. Dost insisted I try some when I told her I was going to look for a book to read. Only I didn't."

"Didn't what?"

"Look for a book. I sat here alone wondering if someone was going to sneak up on me and kill me."

"I told you you don't have to worry about that anymore."

"Yeah. Well, you were a lot more convincing when you told me I did."

"Why didn't you come outside and play like the rest of the kids?" Roxanne's smile would have cheered up a mask of tragedy, but Bats didn't see it. He kept staring at the firelight in the glass.

"I didn't feel like playing. I wanted to think. And you know what a day of thinking has led me to?"

He didn't wait for us to ask.

"It has led me to the conclusion that life is a plot to make you look like a fucking idiot. Then it kills you."

This had the look of a conversation that was headed for places I didn't especially want to go. Hoping against hope, I tried to head him off at the pass. "I must be immortal, then," I said. "With all the times I've looked like an idiot, I should be dead a thousand times already."

Bats looked at me and I knew we were doomed, at least as far as cheerful conversation was concerned.

"That's not what I mean," he said.

I sighed. "What do you mean, Bats?"

"Look at Dost. All this running around, all this building

an empire, all these . . . *trappings*, and what happens? He gets killed by his son for no reason at all.

"Or look at Barry, for God's sake. One of the great corporate empires being built up—for him to have. Anything he could think of to want, in the meantime. Then he goes nuts and he kills his father, gets himself killed, and puts quite a little dent in the empire, too, I wouldn't be surprised. I can't wait to see what Wall Street does when we get out of here and spread the word."

"Neither can your boss," I said.

Bats smiled for the first time. "Ho, ho," he said. He turned to Roxanne. "Haskell went out playing with the kids today, didn't he? Borrowed a pair of skis from the playroom and went skiing, right?"

"I thought he was going to kill himself," Roxanne said. "He kept riding the lift all the way to the top. He seemed scared, just shuffling around up there. He may once have been good enough to do that run—he must have been, considering he got down there twice in one piece—but he's out of practice and out of shape. I tried to tell him, nicely, but he just snarled at me."

Bats nodded. "I will bet you one thousand bucks he took the lift to the top of the mountain to see if he could ski down the other side."

"That would be insane," Roxanne said.

"Depends on your priorities," I said. "He would merely be risking his life. If he gets nailed with a big fine for insider trading, or attempted insider trading, or whatever the hell they want to call it, he might have to sell his *boat*."

"But to hell with Haskell," Bats said. "I was giving you a philosophy lesson, wasn't I?"

"Blefary's *Metaphysics*," I said. "Volume One."

He smiled. "Right, right. As *Blefary* so cogently says, life makes you look like a jerk before it kills you. By this principle, Haskell's on his way out. Of course, so am I."

He was no longer drinking his brandy the way brandy is

supposed to be drunk. Instead of sipping, he was guzzling it like lemonade.

"Aha," I said. "Self-pity. I knew we were building up to something."

Bats looked at me with disdain. "Not just any old self-pity," he proclaimed. "Delayed-reaction self-pity. Life has been planning *my* jerkdom for years."

"Well," I conceded. "Right now, you're *acting* like a jerk."

"Thank you. But you still don't see. Because back at Princeton, I used to lie awake nights wishing I was Barry Dost."

Roxanne said, "Huh?"

Bats looked at her. "Thank you," I said. "I'll treasure that. But you'll notice the limits of my ambition. I wasn't wishing to be Burt Reynolds or Warren Beatty, or whoever else was hot at the time. I mean, I just knew it wasn't possible.

"But Barry and I were both business nerds. Skinny and nearsighted and funny-looking, crazy about sports, and lonely as hell. The only difference between us was that his father had a billion dollars, and my father sold plumbing fixtures.

"But see, that made *all* the difference. I knew that good-looking women would want to sleep with him. I knew he didn't have to worry about finding a job—hell, Barry Dost as an ignominious failure would have a more comfortable life than I would as a wild success."

I opened my mouth.

"Before you say anything," Bats interrupted, "I *know* that Barry's father started with nothing and made that billion. I also know that I could never take the kind of risks it took to make that kind of money.

"So all the time we were hanging around together, being mutual misfits, I secretly hated Barry for being the misfit with the money. The rest of the nerds probably felt the same way about him.

"And Barry had to know it. This was Princeton, after all. We were highly intelligent misfits.

"And he was never anything but nice. I mean, we didn't try to have him bankroll us or anything—I guess he was on a pretty tight allowance, anyway. But he was always willing to do a favor for someone, drop your paper off if you were sick, volunteer to hang around and take messages. All that sort of stuff."

Bats smiled sadly and shook his head. "I remember one night, the Knicks were playing the Sixers at the Spectrum, an important game, and it wasn't on Philadelphia TV. It *was* being televised back in New York, which we couldn't get. So Barry spent the whole day—he cut classes—weaving together this huge network of coat hangers, must have been fifteen feet square. We hung it out the side of the building, hooked it up to the TV, and by God, we got the broadcast from New York. Not great, but passable.

"Barry was good at stuff like that. I suppose he would have been happier as a science nerd, but there was a billion dollars hanging over his head, you know? That we all kind of envied and hated him for."

Bats looked into his glass. When he looked up, his eyes were wet.

"And you know what?" he said. "I don't suppose that poor son of a bitch ever drew a happy breath in his life. He probably stayed awake at night wishing he was me, with a middle-class father who had time for him every once in a while, and no legend to live up to.

"And I never thought of it until this afternoon. After I stopped resenting him, I thought about him like a microscope slide. You heard me the other day, Matt. 'I guess it would drive him crazy.'

"And that, my friends, is why I'm a jerk. Because what drove him crazy was what I envied him for. What I used to curse God for giving him instead of me made him crazy, made him a killer, made him dead. Poor, poor Barry. Poor, poor everybody."

Roxanne spoke softly, comforting him, but I didn't listen. I had a picture in my mind, a huge rectangle of wire hanging out of a dormitory window, defying the limits of ordinary TV. "Barry was good at stuff like that," Bats had said.

Barry, in the wire room, looking down at his father's body.

Barry in the hallway, just before he took the bullets.

"I showed them! I fucking showed them!"

I could go to the wire room anytime. I could go now. But what I really needed to see was the tree. The "coincidental" pine. I ran to the window and pulled a curtain aside. Too late. Pitch-black out there, and a strong wind was crying, on its way to screaming.

Tomorrow would bring rain, the forecast said. But it would also bring daylight, however feeble.

The morning, then. In the meantime, I had a lot to think about.

21

You're right, that's wrong!
—Kay Kyser, "Kay Kyser's Kollege
of Musical Knowledge" (NBC)

The rain came down like a locker-room shower, cold and needle-hard. I was drenched before I even reached the tree.

What I was doing seemed so stupid, I hadn't told anyone except Roxanne what I was up to.

She was disgusted with me. "You won't ski, but you'll do this! You must be nuts."

I tried to reason with her. "Now, Rox, I don't deny it's dangerous—"

"Good!" she said. "Because if you did, you would be *totally* insane. Why can't it wait? Have you looked out the window? It's pouring, for God's sake."

I knew it was pouring. If it weren't raining so hard I could see what I needed to see from my bedroom window.

"Please, Rox, I think I've got this figured out. I've got to go check. We could finish this up today."

"You could finish yourself up today."

"I've got to do this," I told her.

"You're risking your life!"

"But I'm not doing it for fun, okay? I promise I'll be careful."

So I'd gone to the gun room, and I got the lumberjack's strap and a pair of lace-up leather boots, the kind Jack Bromhead had been wearing. I grabbed the strap-on metal teeth that went with the boots, put on a short, hooded yellow slicker, and headed out into the rain.

Trying to look at the bright side of things, I noticed that the wind had died down considerably from last night's gale. And despite the chill of the rain, the air temperature was much higher than it had been. We'd be getting out of here by tomorrow, if this kept up.

I cherished these facts. I hugged them close to myself in an effort to forget what the newly formed slush was doing to my feet. Snowshoes wouldn't have worked on this crud—it was like trying to slog through half-melted sherbet.

I squinted against the rain, keeping my eyes on my destination.

There was something wrong with the tree. I looked at the graying but still unblemished snow at its base and tried to figure out what was bothering me.

It took a few seconds, but I got there. The snow-becoming-slush *was* unblemished. And that didn't make sense. If the blizzard knocked off one small branch of the tree, the windstorm last night should have knocked down dozens. There should be wet black boughs and twigs all around here. It was easy to believe a tree would have a lot of branches that wind and weather could snap off. It was easy to believe it might have none. That it would have one and only one was a little hard to swallow.

I shook my head. Something else to waste time over. So this was the tree in a million that had one weak branch. Worrying about it now would only make me wetter.

I strapped the cleats to my shoes. Then I threw the

broad, rough belt around the tree and clipped it to the metal hooks on the harness around my own waist. Holding the belt by the chains at either end, I flipped my wrists to send it as high up the trunk of the tree as I could reach. Then I pulled my right foot free of the muck it was in, kicked the tree to clear the teeth, dug them into the side of the tree, and started up.

It occurred to me when I was about ten feet off the ground that I should have told Roxanne that I had done this before. For some reason, the colonel who commanded my company decided that MPs should be able to fix their own telephone lines. So we did. Of course, we were going up telephone poles on an army base, which weren't all that high, and which had been climbed so many times already you could almost go up them like a ladder. And we didn't do it much in the cold or the rain.

But we had done it, and I hadn't been too bad. I'd been a whiz at going up. Going up, gravity is your friend. The weight of your body against the strap locks you in place while your feet catch up with your arms. It's just flick and climb, flick and climb, as high up as you want to go.

Coming down was different. You can't really climb down a tall tree. You have to fall down it in a controlled manner, giving in to the great nothingness of space for eternal split seconds until you could use the belt and the cleats to stop yourself again.

If you were a Real Tree Climbing Soldier, by God, you never did stop yourself. You just sort of let the belt slide with enough friction to take you smoothly to the ground without serious bodily harm, kicking the trunk with your cleats every now and then to keep you far enough from the surface to keep from erasing your face against the bark. Or shredding it with splinters against the pole, in our case.

I was sorry I thought that. I dug in the toe cleats and kept climbing. I kept my gaze upward, into the rain. Even when I leaned back against the belt, let go with one hand, and wiped a glove across my eyes to clear my vision, I didn't stop looking into the rain. There's a reason they tell you not to look down.

Flick and climb. Flick and climb.

One of the reasons I was so determined to do this was that for the first time since I'd come to this nuthouse, I actually knew what I was looking for: a piece of cable that stopped at the tree.

Bats's story of the wire-hanger antenna had gotten me thinking, last night. A TV picture (sound, too) was nothing more than the decoding of an electronic signal. As I'd said myself, the playing of a videotape is exactly the same, the decoding of exactly the same signal. The only difference is, it's put directly from the tape machine into the TV set, instead of over the air, to be dragged home by an antenna . . . or even a mesh of coat hangers.

Could you somehow put the signals from a videotape over the air?

You're damned right you could. The Network does it constantly, almost exclusively. All the networks do. Except for sports, news, and some special events, everything you see on television is the output of some videotape machine. Even the filmed shows are transferred to tape before being broadcast.

So it could be done. Could it be done *here?* Halfway up a snowed-in mountain, with no broadcasting facilities within range?

I'd leaned out the window, looking at the wind, and thought about it. Finally, I thought, yeah. Why the hell not?

To hell with broadcasting facilities. To hell with any science-fictional ideas like transmission from a satellite, or anything like that. Hell, satellites are good, but they're not that good. If the Ghost of Dost had come to us via direct satellite transmission, he would have haunted all of northeastern New York and most of western New England.

But none of that was necessary. All it took was one little VCR machine. A VCR machine puts out its signal to your TV with enough juice to overcome electrical resistance in the cable, and to override any interference that might be coming in on the channel you're using for it. In fact, I was sure there was a margin of extra power, because a TV set likes a good strong signal.

But, I told myself, a VCR is just a machine. It doesn't give a damn where it's outputting its power *to*. You press a button that says "play," and the machine says, "Yes, boss," and does its number.

Suppose you didn't hook that output to a TV set? Suppose you hooked it up to some kind of antenna? The signals would still go out, only now they would go out *over the air*, just the way the Network does it. You would have created for yourself your own private, ultra-low-power, extremely illegal, TV station.

Illegal because you need a license to broadcast TV signals. If you hooked your VCR to the antenna on your suburban roof, say, your tape could be picked up by every TV in your house—and probably by every TV in the houses of the neighbors on either side of you, and possibly by your friends across the street.

In the case of a mansion like Rocky Point, you might cover a quarter of the house—a floor or two up or down, and maybe halfway down the corridor. If you planned really well, you'd probably be able to be picked up, hazily, but recognizably, on a TV set that wasn't hooked up to anything at all—its own internal wiring would be enough of an antenna, if you were close enough to the signal.

But then, who *cared* if the reception was bad? How much could people expect from a ghost?

As soon as I had that all worked out, I knew that Aranda was up to something. Her performance was much too good. Those well-rounded, melodic screams to get me to the scene in time to hear Dost "accuse" his son, the convenient collapse, the glib explanations the next morning. Phooey.

The trouble was, try to prove it. Hell, I even knew where the tape of Dost had come from. It was a recorded roll-in to one of those calming-the-animals tapes Barry had finally convinced his old man to make for stockholders and employees. Barry's proudest achievement. The poor bastard.

Once I'd thought of it, it had been undeniable. Dost's attitude hadn't been that of a tormented soul Piercing the Veil, it had been a proud man with stage fright trying to get someone to hold his hand without saying anything that could be construed as weakness.

That was the reason for all the "Why is this taking so long?" business. That explained why he kept calling Barry's name. He wanted his son to reassure him, to tell the big billionaire he wasn't about to make a fool of himself in front of these hot lights and unblinking lenses.

And just try to prove that. That tape had been burned, buried, or thrown off the mountain at the first opportunity. That was one thing I could be sure of.

Flip and climb.

But there was one thing I *could* find. I could find an antenna.

I'd checked this morning. There were twelve cables coming into Rocky Point by the window in the cable room. Even for the kinds of communication a busy businessman needed available, that was a lot of cables. One for TV; one for phone, telex, and fax would do it. Add a couple of back-up cables for each, and you still don't need twelve.

But thirty yards of cable or so would make a dandy antenna for a private, ultra-low-power, extremely illegal TV station.

So I was going to look for a cable that came into the branches and didn't leave them.

Flip and climb.

Now I had reached the first branches. Now I had to do something else I didn't much want to think about. I took a tight grip of one wet bough with my left hand, and threw my right leg over another. Then, with my right hand, I unhooked one end of the tree strap from my harness. I had to go from branch to branch, now. No margin for error.

I had about fifteen more feet to go, which I took about one foot per minute, testing each foothold and concentrating on my grip. One consolation was that it was a little drier up here surrounded by the thick needles.

I only slipped once. "Only." Ha! A branchload of snow, which had managed to hold on through last night's wind, had soaked up enough rain to come loose now. It splattered down through the branches, and hit me with a stinging faceful of slush.

I was startled. I jumped. Big mistake. My cleated feet came away from the tree, and I swiped wildly at my face to clear my eyes. When I could see again, what I was looking at was my boots, and one little tiny broken branch lying on the slush below me. Only then did it occur to me that I was dangling some three and a half stories above the ground by one hand. I found new holds for my hands and feet before that thought even had a chance to register, and stood there in space, hugging the tree as if it were my mother.

Finally, I stopped shaking and clambered up the last few feet to where the wires went through the branches. I got into a position where I could reach them, then reattached the tree strap. Now, not only was the tree my mother, I even had an umbilical attachment to her. It was very comforting.

It didn't take long to spot. Ten wires went right through,

barely brushing branches. An eleventh wire, somewhat closer to the tree than the others, was wrapped twice around a branch, then shot back smartly to the house. Which explained the twelfth fitting near the window at Rocky Point—one going, and one coming.

As I looked at it, though, I wondered why someone had gone through all the trouble to string it back to the house. Not only did that mean you'd have to go to the extra trouble of hauling the returning end up to the window somehow, it wouldn't even help with the TV broadcasting. Signals that get too close together tend to interfere with each other.

It *might* have made sense if the cable had just been tied around the branch with a half-hitch, or even wrapped loosely around, so that it could just be pulled back through the window when it was no longer useful.

But this was wrapped tight, and pulled tight. Looking more closely, I saw that the loops had been lashed together, tied with . . .

I looked again. Tied with *fishing line*.

I started to laugh. In spite of being cold and wet and one more slip from being crippled or killed, I laughed.

Because climbing this tree had been the right thing to do, all right. No doubt about that. I'd just climbed it for the wrong reason.

I stopped and worked it through in my mind, looking for flaws. Nope. It had to be that way. It even explained Barry Dost's dry sleeves against my neck as he choked me. His sleeves had been dry even though he'd been leaning on the windowsill, while everyone else had been soaked, brushing enough snow away to see outside. *That* sill had already been cleaned and now I knew why.

I shook my head. I had risked life and limb in the pouring rain to climb the tree to find evidence of the Great Haunted TV Hoax. But there wasn't any.

What was up here instead was the solution to how G. B.

Dost had managed to wind up so extremely dead up against the rocks that lined his driveway without leaving any tracks. It was as if Columbus had set off looking for America, but had discovered penicillin instead.

It was a messy way to do things, but I was willing to take things any way I got them.

I climbed down to where the branches stopped. Then I carefully lowered myself, arms and legs hugging the tree like a baby bear making his first climb. I worked the tree strap around, and fastened it.

There was a cracking noise. Bark chunked out of the tree and stung my face.

Like an idiot I looked around, but saw nothing.

Two more cracks, and the news sank in—no matter what *I* could see, somebody saw me.

Somebody with a gun.

22

Try not to fall too fast, dear.
—Barbara Luddy, "Winnie the Pooh and Tigger, Too"
(Walt Disney Home Video)

The first thing to do was to get the tree between me and the house. I scooted sideways like a squirrel. Fine. It's always nice to have a couple of feet of wood between you and a rifle.

The only thing I had to worry about now was that he'd shoot the tree strap loose from the chain. Intellectually, I knew that was a long shot. After all, my whole body'd been exposed as a target hung from a branch, and he hadn't managed to hit me. In situations like this, though, your survival instinct tells your intellect to shut the hell up about odds and get us out of this.

The best my intellect could come up with at the moment was a simple proposition: The closer to the ground I was when the belt went, the shorter distance I'd have to fall.

And by God, I'd no sooner thought that than I went down the tree like the best little Tree-Climbing Soldier you ever saw. My sergeant would have been proud. I may have jammed a toe or two in kicking off the tree too hard, and

I may have misjudged the distance at the end slightly and plopped down in a heap into the mud and slush, but at least I was a heap with no extra holes in it. And I had no more dangerous distances to fall.

I felt the cold seeping through my pants, but I didn't care. I threw my head back against the tree and caught my breath. It would have been a good opportunity to think, but there was nothing left to think about.

I knew who was shooting at me. I knew how he'd killed Dost and gotten his body where we'd found it. I knew where Barry fit in. I knew every goddam thing about this case except why anybody was murdered in the first place, and how a DA could possibly make anybody pay for it.

Of course, I could always *ask* why the murder was committed. Assuming, of course, I could get back to the house.

I took a peek around the tree. Nothing happened. I saw that the window of the twelve wires was now closed.

None of which meant anything. A corner of my head made a lousy target. And the window could be closed to make me think I was safe and lure me out in the open for a good shot. How long did it take to open a window?

It was the intellect's turn to tell the survival instinct to take a hike. The situation was so simple, there was no room to figure anything. I either had to make a break for the house or sit here in the slush until I died of pneumonia.

I was tired of getting rained on.

I pushed my back up against the tree and worked myself to a standing position. I took off the tree strap and the hooded jacket. I decided to leave the cleats on, for traction.

It was clearly time to go, but somehow, I couldn't force myself to leave the shelter of the tree. I stood there, trembling, until I got absolutely disgusted with myself for being such a coward.

I said, "Shit," and sprinted away from the tree. Now I *had* to live. I want my last words to be more uplifting than "shit."

More army training. Zig and zag. Don't fall into a pattern. If you fall (and in that mess, boy, did I fall) hit, roll, and come up running.

If any shots were fired, I wasn't aware of them, but then, I had a lot on my mind. I made it to the stoop where Carol, Wilberforce, and I had talked, and scrambled up the stone stairs. I pounded the doorknocker.

Fred Norman answered the door. He looked at me, gave me a look, and stood in my way.

"Let me in," I said.

"You're a mess. What have you been doing out there?"

"Get the hell out of the way."

"My wife works hard to clean this place—"

I punched him in the stomach, then pushed him on his ass when he doubled over. "If you want to give me a hard time," I said, "try to save it for when nobody has been shooting at me for at least an hour or so. Okay?"

Norman groaned.

"I thought you quit, anyway," I said, as I stepped over him. "Where's your nephew?"

Norman kept groaning.

"Okay, maybe I overdid it a little. I've had a bad day. Where's Ralph?"

Norman said, "Kitchen," then began a description of my background, habits, and possible future. It seemed to be doing him good. Certainly his voice was getting stronger as I walked away.

I clanked across the carpet, cursed, then stopped and pulled the cleats off. Then I pounded to the kitchen and stiff-armed the door.

There was no shotgun blast. Instead, there was Ralph, sitting at the table Roxanne and I had shared with Barry the other night. His aunt was sorting through the kitchen cabinets and drawers, putting things in a cardboard box.

Ralph looked up from a cup of hot chocolate. I would have given two years off my life for a cup of hot chocolate just then.

"What the hell happened to *you*?" Ralph demanded.

"I've been out solving our case. And getting shot at."

"And getting mud all over my floors," Aunt Agnes said.

"I thought you quit."

"I've given notice. I'm still on duty here."

"Be quiet, Aunt Agnes," Ralph said. "Shot at? I didn't hear anything."

"I barely did, myself. The noise of the rain would have drowned it out."

"Just what have you solved?"

"Everything."

"Feel like letting me in on it?"

"In a couple of minutes. I want to scrape the mud off me and get some circulation back in my hands and feet. I'd appreciate it if you'd get everyone into the parlor and wait for me."

"Most of them are still asleep."

"Better and better. You won't have to go look for them."

"Yes, sir. As you wish, sir. May I finish my chocolate?"

"Bring it with you."

"You'd better know what you're doing, Cobb," he said.

"I always know what I'm doing," I lied. "Oh, by the way, I slugged your uncle."

"You what?"

"I punched your uncle in the stomach."

Agnes cried, "Fred!" dropped her carton and bolted from the room. If her path had brought her close enough to me, I'm sure she would gladly have stuck a knife in me.

"Why did you punch my uncle?" Ralph said when his aunt had gone.

"Because I wanted to get a wall between me and some

bullets, and he wouldn't get out of the way. Tell him I apologize."

"Oh, that'll make things just great. I've been talking to people. You have a reputation for getting on people's nerves. I can see where it comes from. Did you hurt him?"

"No. I just wanted to move him."

"All right, then," Ralph said. "Let's get going, we're wasting time. And, Cobb?"

"Yes?"

"I hope to God you've really got something. This detective stuff is for *shit*."

Spot wasn't in my room; neither was Roxanne. I made a big deduction: she was in back, walking the dog. I figured that because if she hadn't been, she would have been watching me on the tree, and she would have rushed to my soggy arms the minute I was inside. She would have at least asked me if I was satisfied, now that I'd made frozen mud pie of myself.

Since she hadn't done either of those things, it followed that she hadn't seen me come down the tree, in which case the most likely place for her to be was walking the dog.

I stepped out of my clothes—actually, they were so stiff with snow and mud I practically had to *climb* out—then thawed myself with a quick hot shower. I dressed and ran downstairs.

I was met with universal grousing.

"I thought this was all over with, Cobb," Haskell Freed said.

"I don't care what the sheriff told you," Aranda Dost said. "You are exceeding your authority! You're exceeding decency!"

"Cobb, I demand to know what you think you're doing." Charles Wilberforce stood directly in front of me with his feet planted and his arms folded across his chest, exactly as though I couldn't pick him up and stuff him in my back pocket. Fortunately for him, I'd already had my yearly dose of violence, and I was already regretting it.

"Shut up," I said amiably to one and all. I looked around for Ralph and found him just coming into the room.

"I didn't know how much to tell them," he said, when he saw me surrounded by hostiles, "so I didn't tell them anything."

"Good thinking," I said. "Where's Bromhead?"

What I could see of Ralph's face behind the bandage wore a puzzled look. "I can't find him. I've looked all over. Can't find Roxanne, either, when it comes to that. Or your dog—"

I went cold, colder than I'd been sitting in the snow. Of course, Roxanne would want to see me climb the tree. She was in love with me, right? And what was the best vantage point to see the tree from?

The wire room. Where the shots had come from. I'd sent her right into his arms.

I grabbed Ralph's arms. "Did you check the wire room? The fourth-floor corner, where all the cables come into the house?"

"Yeah. I looked all over."

I turned to Aranda. "Where are they?"

She looked concerned, fluttered her hands. "I—I really don't understand—"

"Aranda," I said quietly. "Don't. Just don't. I know everything, all right? How the body got there. How you worked your husband's ghost trick. It's over. Whatever Bromhead does now will just make it worse."

"Thank God!" Aranda said. "Thank God!" She stood and addressed the gathering. "I'm sorry. I'm so sorry. I want to apologize to all of you." Back to me. "He made me help him. He did. It started as a simple little affair, but he became obsessed. He threatened to kill me if I didn't help him. I didn't really know what he was planning to do until it was too late. I swear—"

Carol Coretti jumped up, grabbed her by the arm and spun her around. "Shut up!" She looked at me. "Can't you tell she's lying? I swear to Christ, how a woman like this can ever fool anybody is beyond me."

"Where are they, Aranda?" I said. "Plenty of time to work on your alibi, later."

"Yes," Carol Coretti said, "and in the meantime, you tell the man what he wants to know."

"But I—I don't *know*!" Aranda struggled to get away, but Carol's red nails dug deeper into her arm.

"Take a guess," I said. "Take a good guess."

Aranda opened her mouth to protest, but Carol spoke first.

"Wait a minute. I owe you one for that business that first night, so I want to tell you this. Whatever happens to Roxanne Schick, happens to you. I'll take care of whatever Cobb leaves. I warn you, he won't leave much. The man's in love."

Wilberforce said, "He's what?"

Carol shook her head. "Men are such idiots." I was impressed. Wilberforce was her boss. Back to Aranda. "Now *where*?"

"I—I guess the garage. I think he's going to try to make a run for it. With the Schick girl as hostage. He was shooting at you. He saw you climbing the tree. That wasn't supposed to happen."

"No," I said, "it sure wasn't."

"Anybody hear them leave?"

"They'd never make it down the mountain in this," Haskell Freed said.

"Shut up," I told him. I was afraid he was right. "Did anybody hear them leave?"

"They can't have left," Aranda said. "The first night Jack put all the cars out of commission. We didn't know that with the blizzard, no one would even try them. He's got to fix one up before he can leave."

All right, then, I thought.

"Ralph, come on. You too, Norman, if you're willing."

I expected more crap from him, but he just looked at me blandly and said, "Sure thing."

"The rest of you," I said, "are deputies. Aranda Dost is the prisoner. If she's not here when we get back, I will personally kill each and every one of you."

As I strode from the room, I heard Haskell Freed saying that my tone was uncalled for, and Bats Blefary telling him to shut up. There was going to be a lot of job changing at the Network when this was over, even without the merger.

Just outside the door, I felt a hand on my back. I turned to see Carol Coretti's bright blue eyes.

"Thanks," I said. "I would have gotten the same information out of her, but it would have taken longer, and been nastier."

Carol showed me a small smile. "God, I feel so *butch*. Aren't you going to get a gun or something?"

I shook my head. "I'm not going to risk getting Roxanne in a crossfire. Spot either, come to that."

"Be careful."

"I intend to. I may be an idiot, but I'm not that big an idiot."

Carol smiled.

"Get back in there now and keep Aranda from putting one over on the rest of the idiots, will you? I've got to get to work now."

"Right. Good luck."

Ralph and his uncle were waiting down the hall. I told them what I wanted.

They didn't like it. "You, the dog, *and* Roxanne are likely to wind up dead," Ralph said.

Fred Norman shook his head. "It's brave, what you want to do, but it's crazy."

"It's the only way," I insisted. "Believe me, if I think he's getting ready to shoot, I'll give him what he wants."

"What if he's ready now?"

"Let's go," I said.

Spot was outside, cowering out of the rain beneath the overhang that protected the walkway from the garage to the house. With his usual puffball of fur now a clinging wet mass, he looked a lot smaller than usual. He seemed glad to see me. I knew I was glad to see him.

"Come on, boy," I said, and stepped out into the rain to the front of the garage.

Spot hung back for a second, giving me a look that said, "What are you, nuts?" Finally, though, training won out over inclination, and he followed me.

Spot and I had to walk to the center of the front door of the building, where a regular person door sat among the sliding doors for cars. I ducked below the windows of the garage doors as we went by. I flattened myself against the wall just to the side of the door, and checked to see if Ralph and his uncle had gotten into position.

They had. It was up to me now.

I threw the door open. I heard Jack Bromhead's voice cursing from inside. "One more goddam minute!"

"Jack?" I said.

"Get the hell away from me, Cobb. I mean it."

"I want to come in, Jack. I want to talk. I'm not armed."

"I am," he said.

"I know. I'm not worried." That was a lie.

"Why not?"

"For one thing, you've got a pretty good idea of what I know, having seen me in the tree. I'm pretty sure you've got Miss Schick in there with you. With that much at stake, you have to know I wouldn't be out here without backup."

"What's the other thing?"

"The other thing is that if you don't shoot any better than you did when I was hanging from the tree, I don't have much to worry about."

Jack started to laugh. "You simple bastard," he said. "I

could have shot you in one earhole and out the other, if I wanted to. The idea was to make you *drop* out of the damn tree, make people think you got careless and fell. I didn't want anybody else looking up there, at least not until I could make myself scarce. Fat lot of good a body full of bullet holes at the base of the tree was going to do me."

"How'd you happen to see me up there?"

"I was looking out the window. I spent a lot of time the last few days looking out that window." There was a spitting noise. "'Can't shoot any better than that,'" he grumbled. "Ha! All right, get in here, if you want to talk."

"I'll come slowly."

"I don't give a damn how fast you come. But God help you if you've got a gun in your hand."

I took a deep breath, held it for a second, then let it go. I stepped through the doorway. Jack Bromhead was straight ahead of me, peeking at me across the nose of his own white Mercedes. He was holding the silver-plated Colt, but it wasn't pointed at me. It was pointed at the windshield in front of the passenger seat of the car, where Roxanne sat.

"I got her tied up and gagged. Don't want you two going all sloppy on me, now."

"That's the least of your problems, Jack," I told him.

"Maybe so," he said. "But since *I've* got the gun, I'm the one who's gonna set the agenda. Gabby used to say that. 'Set the agenda.' I used to tell him to stop trying to sound like somebody who'd been to business school. All right. Keep your hands where I can see them."

Jack stepped out from behind the car. The gun was pointed at me, now. He opened the driver's side door and leaned against it. He held the gun against his body, shifting the muzzle to Roxanne.

"All right," he said quietly. "You wanted to talk. Now talk."

"Suits me fi—" I began.

Jack cut me off. "Oh, if you're figuring on sending your doggie to bite my ass or something, I wouldn't advise it. He's a good dog, and a game rascal, but it'll take him three bounds to get to me, and he'd have a bullet between his eyes halfway through the second. And you'd have one before he hit. If you don't believe me, just give it a try."

"That's not going to be necessary, Jack. I'm counting on your being smart enough to listen to reason."

"Reason," he snorted. "That, my boy, is a word that don't mean anything. Reason is what seems good at the time, then when you look back at it, it don't make any sense. So what's *your* reason going to do for me?"

"Let's give it a try, and see."

"Sure," he said. "Why the hell not? Do you know I was about one minute away from having the rest of these spark plugs in? I would have been out of here in two minutes. Give me a reason for that, I dare you.

"The funny thing is, I thought you were gonna walk in on me when I was taking them out, too. That first night. I was out here fixing things so the cars wouldn't go—waste of time, of course, as it turned out. But who knew the storm was gonna be as bad as all that?" He shook his head. "Anyway, I was out here, and who walks out the front of the house but you and that gal and Wilberforce. What the hell *were* you talking about?"

"Does it matter?"

He waved his gun. "My agenda, remember?"

"We were talking about a sexual pass Aranda tossed at Miss Coretti."

"Why the hell outside?" Jack seemed honestly puzzled.

"Wilberforce was afraid the rooms were bugged."

"Ha. He would, wouldn't he? Nah, we'd never do that. Besides, a lot of people are too good at checking that kind of thing."

"Now, do I get to ask one?"

"Be my guest."

"What was the whole idea of that, anyway? Carol herself swears that Aranda's not gay."

"You want reasons again. The idea was, since Gabby was gonna bite the dust that night, we wanted Aranda to have an alibi. A good alibi, one of your people. We figured it would come out sooner or later that Gabby had talked to his lawyer about getting out of the marriage, so it didn't matter about the unfaithful bit. We'd studied up on everybody, you know."

"I know. That's one of the things that didn't make sense."

"Well, *I* wanted her to make a play for that Blefary geek. He's a bachelor, he's a loner. He rents porno movies. He got in bed with a woman like Aranda, he'd feel like he'd died and gone to heaven; probably give her an alibi even if she *didn't* stay with him all night, which was the plan."

It probably would have worked, at that. "Why didn't she?"

Jack smiled sadly. He shrugged—one shoulder only. The arm that held the gun never moved.

"Aranda didn't want to. Said now that she'd found me, she couldn't stand the thought of any other man being with her."

"But a woman would be okay."

"She said it would be tough, but it wouldn't be the same. Besides, she had this idea that if she spent the night with a lesbian, when you finally dragged it out of her, it would make an even better alibi. Because it was embarrassing, you know?"

"And maybe she was just curious," I said.

Jack's eyes narrowed. "Maybe you're curious to see what a bullet would do to your sweetie, here, huh?"

"Just a thought, Jack," I said.

"Keep the dirty ones to yourself."

I had to cough into my hand to keep from blurting something out. Murder was okay. Treachery was okay.

Using sex to buy an alibi was okay. Sleeping with another woman was dirty. And, since it hadn't worked, Aranda had denied it the next day as a matter of pride. Or maybe to confuse things some more. It had done that.

"You left yourself without an alibi," I said.

"Didn't figure I'd need one. I was Gabby's best friend. And I had the sprained ankle and all."

"Got that sliding down the tree, didn't you?"

"Yep. Stringing the cable for the body trick. God, did *that* go wrong. How'd you figure that?"

"Almost did the same thing myself. When you were shooting at me, remember? Probably would have broken both my ankles if the rain hadn't made the ground soft."

"I didn't have as good an excuse as you. I just slipped the last goddam twenty feet. I used to climb rigs, you know, slick with oil and every other damn thing, but this tree was different. Not enough handholds. Nothing to do but to lace up the boot tight and keep walking on it until the work was done. Of course, that made it a whole lot worse when I finally did ease up on it. If we hadn't been stocked up with pills, I never would have made it."

"You would have been better off if you hadn't."

"Don't say that, boy. When a man decides something, he's got to carry it through, no matter what it is. Gabby— well, I loved him like a brother. But I love Aranda like a woman. Ain't but one woman in a man's life can make him feel the way Aranda makes me feel. That's one time, if he's *lucky*."

"But Dost was getting ready to move on, wasn't he? All you had to do was wait and you and Aranda could be together with no complications."

"Now, that would have been just fine, wouldn't it? Like I was a charity case, needing Gabby's old toys for Christmas, or something. Bad enough folks saying I'm just a hanger-on. I'm a damned good businessman myself, you know. I did my part to make Gabby what he was. More than my part."

"Did you figure this out for yourself, or did Aranda help you to see it?"

"You trying to say she put ideas in my head? No, she didn't. We talked, that's all. Hell, it was a terrible thing for her, too. What would it make her look like to the world, being passed along from man to man like that?"

"So he had to die."

"That's right. I was sorry about it, but I've always been one to face facts."

"You made a plan. You and Aranda."

"Leave her out of it."

"Too late for that, Jack. Besides, the things that have happened here have Aranda's style written all over them."

"What's that supposed to mean?"

"Flamboyant," I said. "Not of This Earth. And deep down, basically stupid."

"It was a good plan," Jack insisted.

I took a step forward. He glared at me, and I stopped. "But it wasn't *your* plan, was it? You would have planned something simple and unprovable, like his falling overboard from a fishing boat or something."

"You don't know what you're talking about," he said.

"Then tell me."

"There's more to these things than you think."

"Not so much. Shall I tell you why you smashed the phone service and put the cars out of commission?"

"Go ahead. You're supposed to be a smart boy."

"Not all that smart. It took me until today to realize it. I kept thinking of Dost in terms of his purchase of the Network. I had all sorts of ideas about people selling Network stock short to make a killing—so to speak—after the news got out about Dost's death. Haskell Freed had even tried to do just that.

"I kept forgetting that Dost's death would affect *dozens* of companies worth billions of dollars. *That's* why it was such a good plan, wasn't it? Some madman would kill Dost, but we'd have no communication with the authorities—"

"Yeah," Bromhead said, suddenly belligerent. "You had a lot of balls telling everybody you'd spoken to the sheriff and he'd made you a deputy. I almost called you a liar to your face."

"That was the idea."

"Yeah. We're just chock-full of ideas, ain't we?"

"You mean you, me, and Aranda? I guess so. So Dost would be dead, and nobody would know about it. So you'd have, what? A day? We'd probably wait a day before we tried to walk to town."

"That's what we figured. It's a good four hours' walk to the bottom of this mountain even if it didn't snow, the way the road curves and all. And the weather forecast called for *some* snow. We didn't know we were gonna get a whole winter's worth all at once."

"So there would be at least a day for the people you had fronting stock for you to sell your interests in Dost's various businesses. You'd have an enormous amount of cash."

"Enormous is right." Jack shook his head at the size of it.

"Then, when the news of his death came out, and the price of the stock crashed—all of it, not just the Network stock—you'd be in a position to buy it all back."

"No, son. Not all of it. That's the point. I'd have enough cash to buy up the businesses it made sense for me to run. The drilling-tool company we started out with. The trucking firms. That kind of thing. What the hell do I care about cupcakes, or television, or any other of the damn-fool things Gabby got himself involved with?"

"Of course, you'd still have a lot of money left, to keep Aranda happy. The kind of *bono* she'd grown used to."

"I told you to stop that."

"Was it always the idea to frame Barry? I suppose it was. Aranda and he never did get along. Did you know of the legal angles Wilberforce came up with? I mean, did you hope to get the whole thing legitimately? Then you could sell off what you wanted, and never have to worry about any stock manipulations at all."

I scratched my chin. "Nah. I don't think so. Your mind doesn't work that way, and I don't think Aranda's smart enough. I think Barry was always scheduled for the squeeze, though. I hope your original plan was something better than that bogus TV business. How did you ever let her force that one on you?"

Jack took a tighter grip on the handle of the pistol. He wanted to shout, but choked it off. In a strained voice, he said, "You seem to be forgetting, while you keep insulting my woman, that I've got yours trussed up like a prize fowl in here, with a gun aimed at her belly."

I hoped Roxanne would forgive what she was going to hear next. "What is this 'my woman' stuff? You tried to kill me, Jack. That makes it me and you. The rest of the world can take their chances."

"Don't try to bullshit me, Cobb."

"Didn't Dost's famous reports say it was a big mistake to piss me off?"

"They said that. They also said you were tight with Miss Schick, and that you'd undoubtedly try to call her once a day to see how she was holding up under the strain of selling the family business."

I said nothing. The reports were probably right.

"Hell," Jack said. "That's why we sent the poison-pen letters. To get *you* up here. If you couldn't get in touch with your people, you'd start *looking* at things. We didn't want to risk what you might turn up."

"*That* sounds like Aranda."

"It was a damned smart idea," Jack proclaimed.

"It was a ridiculous long shot."

"It worked, didn't it?"

"It got me up here, alert, and suspicious. All you'd have

to do is get one of your lawyers to tell Tom Falzet you wanted me up here to talk about confidential things we've got going in Special Projects, to see if you wanted to continue them once the sale went through. I wouldn't have been as ready for trouble. I might have missed things I noticed. You might have gotten away with this, if Aranda hadn't planned a murder like it was one of those New Age parlor tricks."

"All right!" Jack took the gun off Roxanne and pointed it at me. "All right. I've had about enough of you. You just back on out that door. Nice and slow, don't trip. Take your doggie with you."

"What's the brilliant plan?" I asked.

He stuck his arm straight out as if to fire. I didn't flinch as much as I might have because fear made it impossible for me to move.

Jack didn't know that. "One thing I've got to say for you, Cobb, you got guts."

Sure, I thought, the contents of which had come very close to landing in my shorts.

"The brilliant plan is this," he went on. "I am going to take Miss Schick out of the car again, and have her by me while I finish getting this car running. Then she and I will drive out of here, unmolested. I should have a decent head start. It will take you awhile to find the spark plugs for the other cars."

"And you and Miss Schick plunge to your death off the side of the mountain."

"Just taking our chances, like you said. Now get."

"As you leave the woman you love holding the bag."

"She'll be fine. There's no evidence against her."

"Which means she suckered you into doing all the dirty work."

"I keep telling you to shut up, boy. You don't seem to be listening."

"How long do you think it's going to take her to sell you out?"

Jack spat. "This has all been planned for, Cobb. You don't get to be as old as I am without learning some plans fall apart."

"It's been planned for, all right. Aranda's just got a different plan. She's singing like a canary—of course, she's a professional singer, so what the hell—about how you forced her into everything. 'Terrorized' her was the word, I think."

"You're lying, you son of a bitch. All she has to do is be quiet—"

"Right, and meet you in Brazil when the heat is off."

A voice outside said something.

I called back over my shoulder. "Is that you, Fred?"

"Costa Rica," Fred called back. "She was babbling on while you were talking to the red-haired gal. He's supposed to go to Costa Rica. She said Jack has a disguise and a fake passport and another car and God knows what all in a cabin about twenty miles north of here. Stuff they set up in case something went wrong. That fellow Bats was writing it all down when we came out here."

I turned to Jack Bromhead. "So that's the answer to my question. She sold you out before you could even think. And screwed up your getaway plans, even if you *could* get down the goddam mountain."

Jack reached into the car and pulled Roxanne roughly across the seat. He kept pulling, and she fell to the concrete floor of the garage. He dragged her to her feet.

"Go on," he said. "Get out of here. Go on, I didn't tie your feet. Beat it!"

"Come on, Rox," I said.

Her eyes were wide and frightened above the gag. "It'll be all right," I said. "Ralph will get you loose. I love you."

She mumbled something into the gag. I patted her on the back and she went.

Jack pointed the .45 at me again. "You stay."

"I wasn't going anywhere."

"You wouldn't even let me have this, would you? You had to destroy what was left. *I saved your life,* you ungrateful son of a bitch!"

True, I thought, although at the same time, he'd preserved his various plans from whatever Barry might have told me about them.

I didn't say that. Instead, I said, "I'm not really sure what you're talking about, Jack."

"Well, how big an asshole do you think I am? I *know* there's no way down this mountain without getting killed! I was gonna let the gal off at the edge of the property and try my luck, that's all. She would have got a little wet. I wasn't even gonna leave her tied up."

He started to cry. "Don't you ever go scoffing at this supernatural stuff, because I swear, Aranda's a witch. She's no damn good. I knew she was no damn good from the minute I laid eyes on her. I was around her for years, you know, but the minute Gabby started getting tired of her, she had me the way the snake gets a rabbit.

"I am in love with that evil creature. I am a fool, I have been a fool, and I continue to be a fool—look at me, crying like a little boy. I killed my best friend because she wanted it that way. I killed a boy I used to build kites for.

"I could do it, because I got real good at lying to myself. That's all I was going to have, Cobb. Her body for a while, more money than anybody sane could ever have a use for. And the lies that made it all seem to make sense. The 'reasons.' Remember what I said about reasons.

"Then you came along and ruined me. When I came into this garage, all I had left was the lies. But you fixed it so I couldn't even *pretend* to believe them anymore.

"So I want you to see this. Remember it, if you ever fall in love with a witch."

The gun came up, past my face, to his right temple.

I yelled "No!" and ran at him. I'd forgotten to give Spot his command, but the Samoyed jumped him, too.

Jack didn't really want to die. If he had, he would have just pulled the trigger, and I might have reached him in time to catch his corpse as it hit the ground. As it was, he wavered, trying to figure out whether to shoot Spot, me, or himself. In the end, he shot only a hole in the garage roof as we knocked him over.

There was a struggle. The gun went flying. I got on top of him, and things were going fine, until he kneed me in the groin.

That's something it takes a more determined man than I am to ignore. First came the pain, then the nausea, then the panic at the idea that you might have just been whistled out of the gene pool. Men will know what I'm talking about. Women will have to take my word for it.

By the time I quit rolling around on the concrete and decided I was going to live, after all, Jack had jumped up and scuttled along between the noses of the parked cars and the wall of the garage to another door.

I'd have to talk to Ralph and Fred. Neither of them had mentioned another door to the garage. If they had, one of them could have been covering it.

I tried to yell to them that Jack had gotten loose and was now behind the house, but my voice came out a strangled groan. I swallowed, tried again, and managed to make sounds that would pass for human speech. I got to my feet and took off after him.

The second most amazing thing about a shot to the balls (the first most amazing thing is how much it hurts), is how quickly it goes away. If you're not seriously injured, you're generally good as new (if warier) as soon as you get your breath back.

Once again, I plunged into mud and slush.

When I caught up to him, Jack Bromhead was standing

on the wall behind the house, trying to get up enough nerve to jump.

"Don't do it, Jack." I said it quietly—I didn't want to startle him.

He kept looking down at the face of the cliff. "Why the hell not?" he asked.

"Because you won't fall clean. It'll hurt like a bastard. You'll be flayed alive against the rocks. Two, once you jump, you can't change your mind, but I'll bet you'll sure want to."

"I'd take that bet, if I was gonna be around to collect." He still wasn't looking at me.

"Three, if you jump, some poor deputy sheriffs or state troopers are going to have to risk their lives to bring your worthless carcass out of there again."

Jack stood there for a long time with the rain beating down on him. I heard Ralph and Fred and Roxanne come out of the garage, but I waved frantically behind my back for them to stay where they were.

Finally, Jack said. "Yeah. I guess enough is enough." He looked over his shoulder at me, and began to turn around.

And his sprained ankle gave way.

It looked at first as if he'd gone through a trapdoor. By the time I finished gasping, though, I realized he hadn't disappeared completely. The upper part of his body had shot in the opposite direction from his feet, and had landed on the top of the wall. Through the wet snow there, I could see the top of Jack's head, and his hands grasping for purchase against the rock.

I could also see he was slipping.

I was already running toward the wall. It was hard going through the mud, and Jack was slipping farther into oblivion by the second. I got there just as his grip gave way. I jumped up, reached over, and caught the neck of his jacket just before he disappeared.

A soaking-wet man is heavy. For a long, long moment, I

felt my own feet coming clear of the ground. I had to brace one hand against the wall to keep from being pulled over.

"Try to climb up," I said.

"Yeah," Jack said.

The trouble was, the way I had him, I was pulling his head right into the wall. There was no way he could climb up, and no way I could change my grasp.

I squeezed my eyes shut and concentrated all my strength into my right wrist and hand.

I didn't know how much longer I could do this. There was a roaring in my ears and a pain up my arm that made the knee in the groin a fond memory.

Through the roaring, I could hear a voice screaming at me to let go. I resisted to the limit of my will for an eternity of fifteen seconds. Then it occurred to me it might not be a demon urging me to let the man die.

I opened my eyes. It was Ralph Ingersoll. He and Fred each had one of Jack's arms. If I let go, they could easily pull him to safety.

I was delighted to let go.

Ralph and Fred heaved, and Jack tumbled to the snow at our feet.

I looked at him while I flexed my fingers and worked my arm.

"Should have let him fall," Fred Norman said.

Jack showed no reaction. He was breathing. He lay on the ground like a dead man. His face was as dead as any bullet could have made it.

"Come on," I said. "Let's get him into the house."

23

On with the show, this is it!
—Mel Blanc, "The Bugs Bunny Show" (ABC)

I turned on the "haunted TV," which was still hooked up to nothing but the power supply, and immediately was presented with the image of Wile E. Coyote falling two million miles or so into some desolate western canyon.

I gave a bitter little laugh. Roxanne had picked the video tape from Barry Dost's collection. It was a shame, I thought, that Aranda and Jack weren't here to see it, especially Jack. They were locked securely in separate top-floor rooms, guarded by Ralph and his Uncle Fred.

I'd already explained to the rest of the gang how the bogus haunting was done, and the thinking that led me there.

Bats Blefary, perhaps because he remembered Barry doing this kind of thing, had the easiest time catching on.

"All right," he said. "All you need is the VCR and something to use as an antenna. But if the cable you climbed the tree to find out about isn't the antenna, what is?"

"Something a lot better," I said. "And a lot closer.

Something made of nearly as much uninsulated wire as Barry's web of coat hangers."

"Cobb," Wilberforce warned me, "you are making mysteries to no purpose."

I supposed he had a point. I sighed and went on. "It's a bed. Jack Bromhead's antique boardinghouse nightmare, with the metal bedstead and the open box spring. There was a piece of dipole antenna wire in his closet." It would be evidence in Jack's trial, I supposed. Jack had said all the evidence would point to him. "A piece of antenna wire," I went on, "just long enough to reach from the VCR in Jack's room to his bed, with the insulation already skinned back at the ends to make it easy to hook up.

"I've got to give him credit for nerve," I said. "They had the scam set up, and Aranda was screaming to get us all on the scene. Jack Bromhead's room is the one just below this one. He poked his head out to ask me what was going on. If I'd stopped for a chat and leaned against his door, I would have seen what was going on. It must have given him quite a scare to see Barry, back from hiding, rushing upstairs right behind me. That might have blown everything right there, but they got lucky. Barry made two mistakes, then: he was cryptic about the trick, and he thought I was in on it somehow."

"It seems to me that shotgun was a mistake, too," Haskell Freed said. "It gave Bromhead a chance to shoot him down before he could say anything more."

"True. Of course, once they showed the tape, Barry had to die in any case. I suspect they hoped he'd disappear again. Then they could try to find him and finish him off in some way that looked like suicide."

Carol Coretti shuddered, but she wasn't chilled enough to forget she was a lawyer. "You just suspect this?"

I shrugged. "Jack has gone mute, and Aranda won't say anything but it was all Jack's fault. By now, she'll be ready to swear that Jack killed Cock Robin."

Another cartoon had started. The coyote (*Stupidicus maximus*) was back, none the worse for the catastrophes that had befallen him in the last cartoon, still trying for the Road Runner.

I leaned out the doorway and called, "That's enough, Rox!" To the rest of the gang I said, "Now I'll show you how the body got out there."

Roxanne joined us, and we went down the hall to the wire room.

Earlier, Ralph and I had commandeered some supplies from Aunt Agnes's kitchen, specifically, a one hundred-pound sack of long-grain rice and one broom handle. Fred had cut the broom handle to a convenient length, and we'd poked it through the top of the rice bag, just below the seam. It was waiting for us in the wire room. We'd also taken the surf-casting rod from the tackle room and cut loose the tangle.

"Now, some of this I know for sure; some of it is my best guess, okay?"

"Why are you doing this?" Wilberforce demanded. "Why don't you wait and make these demonstrations for the police, when they get here."

"Because I want *you* people convinced. Prudence demands we spend at least the rest of today and tonight here. That means we are *de facto* jailers for two very dangerous people. Again, tomorrow, if it is tomorrow, when we leave, we have to get them to the sheriff."

I'd wanted to save this speech for the end of the demonstration, but what the hell. I looked at each of them in turn. "None of us is a professional at this. That means we're going to have to help each other all we can. I want you all to be as sure as possible that we're doing the right thing."

I got nods in reply. Fine with me.

"All right then," I said. "When everyone went to bed, Jack sneaked out to disable the cars. He waited for

Wilberforce, Ms. Coretti, and me to go back inside, then went to Dost's room and woke him, if he had to. Part of Dost's legend was that he'd just as soon work as sleep. Anyway, Jack said he had some business thing to talk about. Dost was always ready to talk business. Maybe he said it was something they should talk over with Barry—that would be a good way to get him to the wire room—Barry's room is right next door.

"I know my name came up in conversation, because Barry heard his father saying it. That's why he suspected me.

"Anyway, Jack gets Dost in here and beats his head in with something. Take your pick. There's a modern sculpture in each of the finished bedrooms that would do just fine. Dost falls. There he lies."

Agnes Norman gave a little scream. All eyes followed my finger to the bag of rice.

"Actually, this is a little light to be Dost's body, but it will do. I'm going inside now. I hope you can all see."

I went to the panel just inside the window, and pulled loose the dummy cable. I had checked earlier—there was plenty of slack, the extra having been tucked into the panel box. I took the end of the cable over to the bag.

I slapped my hand down on the brand name painted on the bag. "This is Dost's chest," I said. "And the broom handle is his arms. All I do then is run the cable across his chest a couple of times, then around under his arms. Then, after I make sure everything is tight enough so that he won't slip out by his own weight, I tie everything off here behind his head with a knot called a sheep shank. Any Boy Scouts in the audience?"

"Girl Scout," Carol Coretti said. I asked her to tell me about a sheep shank.

"It's a very strong knot with a free end. If you pull the free end, the knot comes loose."

"Exactly. Next, I get some good strong fishline, which I

pull off the reel, cut, wrap a few times around something sturdy, like this pipe, then tape securely to the free end of the cable." I used black electrician's tape, of which there were several rolls in a toolbox.

"What I *don't* want to do," I said, "is, in getting the line the right length, or cutting free a tangle, to somehow drop a little piece of the fishline on the body, where it can get caught in the clothes, and be found near the body later. Which Jack Bromhead unfortunately did."

I lifted the rice up by the long end of the cable. The knot held. "You will notice," I said, "that the cables dig into the sack. This would cause bruises across the chest, and on the back, angling up toward the neck. There wasn't enough of Dost's chest left to check, but Ralph and I did find bruises just like that on his back. I had a wild idea of the man's beating himself, but it didn't really suit him. This makes a lot more sense."

I told them that they might want to watch what happened next from a window, either from Barry's room next door, or the room next to that. The crowd dispersed. I opened the window of the wire room and got rained on, but I was used to that.

"All I have to do now is to get the body to the window-sill, inevitably cleaning it of snow in the process . . ." I grunted as I did it—my arm still hurt from catching Jack.

"Then give it a little push."

That's what I did. The sack dropped about five feet straight down, until the slack was taken up, then it started to swing on the pivot of the branch. It went faster and faster until it bottomed out, but even then it didn't slow down. The kinetic energy would have kept it swinging upward, the way a watch on a chain would. I didn't think the rice (or Dost) had enough kinetic energy to swing all the way around, but it was theoretically possible.

Before we had to worry about any theoretical possibilities, though, the fishline pulled taut, the sheep shank came free, and the cable unwrapped from the bag-body, which at that second was keeping a high-speed rendezvous with the rocks. Rice sprayed everywhere. I heard gasps and screams from the other rooms.

"Keep watching," I said. I began pulling in the fishing line, hand over hand. The black end of the cable seemed to twitch, like the head of an impossibly long snake, lunging slowly from the tree toward the house. I pulled it the rest of the way in. It tangled the fishing line, but who would be suspicious of a fishing line? When I had the cable close enough to the window, I grabbed it, took off the tape, and reattached it to the panel board.

I joined the rest of them in Barry's room. "If you do it right," I said, "you don't leave a mark on the snow."

Roxanne was shaking her head. "I'm sorry I saw the rice bag hit," she said. "I have too good an imagination. He did that to his best friend. Why didn't you let him jump, for God's sake?"

I turned to the group. "Any other questions?"

24

Works for me.
—Fred Dryer, "Hunter" (NBC)

Three days later, Roxanne sat with her head on my shoulder as an Amtrak train brought us southward. Spot slumbered peacefully (and illegally) at our feet. I would have been just as glad to rest my head on hers and go romantically to sleep, but she kept asking questions.

I really couldn't blame her—we hadn't been able to speak to each other for a couple of days. When our caravan reached the sheriff's office in town (Fred Norman had found the spark plugs) the sheriff, a gray-haired old guy named Mallin whose beer belly did not disguise the iron underneath, immediately ordered two things. First, he sent one of his men with the medical examiner up to Rocky Point to see if there actually were two bodies up there. Second, he took everybody into custody.

By late afternoon, he had thrown back most of the catch, retaining only Jack and Aranda—and Ralph and me.

I was charged with obstruction of justice, impersonating an officer, interfering with a crime scene, being a general pain in the ass, and mopery with intent to gawk. The charges against Ralph were similar.

Wilberforce had been outraged. He had been so outraged, and had raised such a stink, he pissed off the sheriff so much that Mallin kept us in custody until the very last second he legally could without going for an actual indictment.

In the meantime, the medical examiner had come back with the bodies and the Normans and the Network people (including Wilberforce) had been questioned and allowed to go home. Aranda had started accusing me and Ralph of raping her. Jack had started to talk.

Roxanne had stayed behind at the local Quality Inn, fending off reporters, getting Ralph and me a local lawyer, and just generally behaving the way the girl of your dreams would in circumstances like that.

Finally, Sheriff Mallin had formed a pretty good idea of what had happened, and he let us go.

"I suppose I ought to thank you," he said as he unlocked my cell. His face did not seem to be filled with gratitude.

"Don't mention it," I said.

"You'll be back up here for the trial," he said. "All you out-of-town people will be back here for the trial. One for him, and one for her, if we can get him to blow the whistle on her under oath. If he don't, she could be sitting a lot prettier than she deserves."

"He'll open up," I said. "Jack's getting used to the idea of just how big a fool he's been. He won't let Aranda walk away from this."

Mallin grunted. "We'll see. Anyway, the trial is the only time I ever want to see you again. Don't come up here on no ski trips. What's so goddam funny?"

Roxanne and I had decided to hop the train on its way down from Montreal because it was slow, and because we hadn't had a chance to talk since I'd been arrested.

"Do you think he did it on purpose?" she asked.

"Of course he did it on purpose. He rigged the cable, he set up the murder—"

"Not Jack. Wilberforce. Do you think he gave the sheriff a hard time so he would keep you in jail longer?"

I laughed. "I hadn't thought of it, but now that you mention it, I'm sure that's why he did it."

"Do you want me to get him fired?"

"Huh?"

"Well, it looks like I'm stuck with being the Network's biggest stockholder. Maybe it's time to get involved. Do you want to be president of the Network or something?"

"No, I do not. And if you think I got into this . . . *relationship* for you to *buy* me things, the Network or anything else, we can call the whole thing off right now."

She showed me an impish smile. "Just reminding myself why I love you," she said. "I had a few doubts when you as much as told Jack Bromhead to go ahead and kill me."

"Didn't fool him for a second," I told her.

"He wasn't tied up and gagged. But you know, I never did think he was going to kill me."

"I'm glad," I said. "No, the only one you have to fire because of this is Falzet's secretary. Turns out *she* was Dost's inside source."

"Matt, they really were stupid, weren't they? Jack and Aranda?"

"Almost unbelievably stupid," I acknowledged. "There were any number of fairly safe ways they could have done away with Dost. But that wasn't enough for Aranda—she had to fix Barry, too."

"But how could they have foreseen . . . ?"

"That's the point. The didn't foresee a single damn thing, but they went ahead with the murder anyway."

"But *why?*"

"They were psyched. Mallin sort of accidentally left a copy of Jack's statement on his desk when he went to get my stuff, so I know what they *thought* they were doing. The idea was, snow or no snow, they'd screwed their courage to the sticking place, and if it came loose now, they'd never get it back. So even when the snow turned out to be six times worse than expected, they went ahead and killed Dost, anyway."

"But what was the point of moving the body away from the house? Why make an impossible crime out of it?"

"It wasn't supposed to be an impossible crime. It was supposed to be a crime that took place away from the house. The forecast was for only about five or six inches, remember. That would have left the tops of the black rocks uncovered. The idea was that Dost was meeting someone secretly outside for some shady reason, and that he and the person he was meeting had walked on the rocks so as not to leave tracks. Jack had, apparently, already put some recognizable scuff marks on tops of some of those rocks, using a pair of Dost's shoes, and a pair of Barry's."

"So they were going to frame Barry all along."

"Right. They'd even set up some of the financial chicanery their people in New York were pulling to look as if *Barry* were the one who'd planned to cash in on his father's death."

"But they didn't figure on the snow," Roxanne said.

"Right. They also didn't figure on Dost hitting the rocks and busting like a water balloon, either. Or Barry going quite as crazy as he did, and disappearing until the worst possible moment. I mean, as far as Jack was concerned it turned out to be the *best* possible moment, but he couldn't have know that."

"What about the television-set business?"

"Ah. Jack didn't come out and say this, but I suspect it was directed at me, personally. Ralph and I had scoffed at the supernatural earlier. Got pretty giggly about it. Aranda was peeved. I guess she wanted to rub my nose in it. It wouldn't do Barry any good, and it would Teach Cobb A Lesson. Once again, they didn't expect Barry, who'd shown them how to do the trick in the first place, to show up and go into hysterics. They just figured that since they'd pulled off a frightening, impossible crime, why not milk it?"

"Even their original plan was pretty dumb."

"What's harder to understand? The smart things people do, or the stupid things?"

"Good point."

"Thank you. Besides, I think deep down, Jack wanted to be caught."

Roxanne looked at me with the same penetrating gaze she'd used on the night of the inquisition. "What do *you* want, Cobb?"

"What?"

"You don't want to be president of the Network; what do you want?"

"I want a vacation. A nice, long vacation. Just me and you. And Spot."

Her face lit up. "You really mean that?"

"Hoo boy, do I mean it. Think you can arrange it with the higher-ups, O mighty stockholder?"

"Piece of cake," she assured me.

"Good. Can I get some sleep now?"

"In a minute. One more question."

I sighed. "Let's have it."

"Why didn't you let Jack kill himself?"

"Ah," I said.

"I mean, you set that woman up . . ."

"So why did I twice keep Jack from punching his own ticket? Well, he did save my life, you know."

"He's the one who put your life in danger in the first place!"

"He could have let Barry kill me, first."

"Then he wouldn't have had you around to say he saved your life!"

"Good point," I conceded. "Then there's the idea that

maybe, though I don't really have any qualms about screwing over a murderer any way necessary, I don't especially like to picture myself as a roving executioner, even at second hand."

"Keep talking."

"Don't like that one, huh? Maybe I'm so brilliant that I saw through the legal ramifications of what I had, and I realized that if Jack died, Aranda would probably walk. Not that her conviction's a sure thing, even now, but at least there's a chance. *She* became the murderer I had to screw over, and a living Jack Bromhead was the only means of accomplishing that."

I shrugged. "The truth's in there somewhere. I'm damned if I know exactly what it is, though. Does it matter?"

"Not to me," she said. "I'm kind of glad you saved him, no matter what I said."

"Good. Happy now?"

"I probably could be, if you'd put your arm around me."

"Like this?"

"Mmmm," she said, and cuddled closer. The train rocked us to sleep.